Second Chances 101

Second Chances 101

Donna K. Weaver

Emerald Arch Publishing

ISBN Paperback: 978-0-9899928-6-2
ISBN Ebook: 978-0-9899928-7-9
ISBN Audiobook: 978-0-9899928-8-6

Published by Emerald Arch Publishing

The Ripple Effect Romance Series

Like a pebble tossed into calm water,
a simple act can ripple outward
and have a far-reaching effect on those we meet
perhaps setting a life on a different course—
one filled with excitement, adventure,
and sometimes even love.

Other Works by Donna K. Weaver

Safe Harbors Series

A Change of Plans (#1)
Hope's Watch (#1.5)
Tom Canvas (#2)
A Season of Change (#2.5)

A Savage Ghost

Waves of Deceit (coming January 2017)

One

rancie placed flowers on the grave and stepped back. Since the burial two months ago, she had come every Sunday, the only day she had off from both her jobs. She didn't really know why she still did it. Maybe it was the feeling that people who had known her and Greg would expect it. They had all thought the marriage was a good one in spite of his bad health. It had all been a lie.

At the sound of approaching footsteps, Francie glanced over her shoulder. She turned, a smile replacing her earlier frown.

"Hey, Ma," Rafe said, coming to stand beside her.

"Hi." She smiled up at her only child, feeling a powerful sense of gratitude that something good had come from Greg. Rafaele had his father's height and light eyes, but he had gotten his dark hair, olive complexion, and slender frame from her. She said a silent prayer that life wouldn't turn Rafe into the bitter, spiteful man his father had become.

"You shouldn't come here." Rafe shoved his hands in his pockets. "He didn't deserve it."

"I thought you were going to pack today." Francie wasn't going to argue with him. She had given up trying to stop Rafe from making disparaging comments about his father, but she refused to acknowledge them.

"Done. I have to talk to you though."

Something in his tone made Francie turn to face him. She crossed her arms but dropped them almost immediately. After Rafe had taken a psychology class and studied body language, he had harassed her for doing it, saying that it was a sign she was closed up. She would have reminded him that she was the parent, but his harshest comment had been that she only dropped her arms at home when she was doing something with them. Francie might have been able to keep her problems from their neighbors, but Rafe had lived the truth.

Her little protector, now all grown up.

"Let's sit down." Rafe guided her to a stone bench not far from the grave.

He sounded so serious that Francie's stomach twisted. Her biggest fear was that he would make the same mistakes she and his father had. Greg had been so handsome in his cap and gown, so confident. They were going to conquer the world, and Francie had believed every word of it. College, great jobs. They were going to have it all. She clenched her rough, callused hands and took a deep breath, trying to steel herself for bad news, clinging to Rafe's comment that he was packed.

"I don't like leaving you alone like this." He leaned forward, his hands on his knees, not looking at her. "I don't have to go, you know."

"You will stop talking nonsense." Francie shifted so she could face him, her poor heart thudding. All these years of working two jobs so he could have the best opportunities—and he might throw them away because of *her*? "Getting that scholarship to Harvard is as much my reward as yours. They don't give out many of those each year."

2

"You think I don't know that?" Rafe sat up, scowling. "Look, Ma—"

"No." Francie crossed her arms. "I don't need anyone's help."

"That's the problem. You've done it all for too long." Rafe jumped to his feet and strode to the grave, glaring at it. "And all those years, taking that, that—" He bit back the word and kicked at the flowers instead.

Francie let Rafe rant. Once he had calmed down—and he always did—she could reason with him. He finally gave the flowers one more kick and turned to her.

"It makes me sick to think of leaving you here alone."

"Oh, really?" She indicated the grave. "Let's be real here. It would have been easier for you to leave me alone with *him*?"

Rafe dropped onto the ground in front of the bench and ripped out a clump of grass. She slid off the seat and sat beside him, their shoulders touching. When she didn't say anything, he stopped mangling the lawn and leaned his head on her shoulder.

She blinked back sudden tears; he couldn't see her cry. Rafe could be so stubborn. If he got it in his mind that staying in Boone with her was the right thing to do, he would. Even if it meant giving back the prestigious scholarship.

"Have you decided what you're going to do?" Rafe finally asked, lifting his head.

"I have." Francie had been hoping for this question. She reached into her purse and removed an envelope.

"What the—" Rafe said, when he read the return address. He took out the letter and gave it a quick scan. "Appalachian State? Sweet! When did you apply?"

"When you applied to Harvard. Same with the scholarships."

Rafe leapt to his feet. "You got a scholarship?"

"No scholarship for me." Francie tugged on the leg of

his jeans, the ratty condition making her grimace. He was saving his new clothes for school. When he finally stopped in front of her, Rafe ran a hand through his short, dark hair. Confused by his expression, she asked, "Are you upset about this?"

"No." Rafe reached for her hands and pulled her to her feet. "I'm ticked because you didn't tell me about it sooner."

"I wasn't sure they'd accept me." Francie looked at the grave to the side. "You had enough on your mind about your own application. I didn't want you to worry about mine."

"But I thought Dad's life insurance only paid off his medical bills. How are you going to pay for your tuition?"

"I've applied for a job on campus, a full-time one." Francie reached up and straightened his hair. "If I get that, the benefit will be three quarters of my tuition. Grants will cover the rest."

"Ma." Rafe grabbed her hand and held it against his chest. "It doesn't add up. Full-time work plus full-time school plus studying? You won't have time to work a second job. How will you live?"

"Who do you think you are?" Francie jerked her hand back. "Your father?"

"Don't be insulting." Rafe's eyes flashed.

"I'm sorry. It's just that an eighteen-year-old boy shouldn't have to be worrying about his mother."

Rafe's face softened. "We're in this together, remember? Isn't that what you've always told me? You know I won't be able to concentrate if I'm worried about whether or not you have enough food to eat and decent clothes to wear."

"See what I mean? That's *my* line." Francie picked up her purse and the letter Rafe had dropped. What would she have done all these years without him? She took his arm and led him toward her old clunker. "Look, I've got a good counselor, and she's full of ideas. Since I'm a new student I'll be taking low-level general ed. classes this first year." She sighed. "Including remedial math."

Rafe's bicycle leaned against the old Reliant K car her Granny Gladys had left Francie the year before, along with the house. The only way Francie had survived the last nineteen years had been with the old woman's quiet, unassuming help.

"You want to ride with me?" Francie asked, when Rafe pulled his helmet from the handlebars.

"No, I've got a date."

Francie forced her expression to stay neutral. She remembered what it had been like at his age. If her parents hadn't put up so much resistance to her marrying Greg, she probably wouldn't have rushed into it right after graduating from high school. Yet, looking at her tall son, Francie knew she could never regret that decision. It had given her Rafe.

"Want to take my car?" she asked with an almost-sincere smile.

Rafe put on the helmet and threw a well-muscled leg over the bar. "Really?" He gave her his typical you-didn't-just-say-that look. "*You*? On *my* bike?"

"You won't be out late, will you?"

"Love you, Ma." Rafe rode away.

Francie sighed and unlocked her door. Why hadn't she realized that her son becoming an adult didn't mean she would stop worrying about him?

Alex paused before entering the breakfast nook. Sam was already at the table, sipping a cup of herbal tea. He could tell it wasn't going to be a good day. His daughter's dark strawberry blond hair hung greasily—from product and not from a lack of hygiene—around her shoulders, highlighting the black makeup that filled the entire eye socket area. She had a light coating on her face of what had to be white greasepaint. A white lace choker accented the black, sleeveless, pseudo-leather bodice.

He closed his eyes, not wanting to see anymore. The image of the sweet little girl who had once come running to throw her arms around his neck filled his mind. That was when he had liked coming home from work. How had he screwed up so bad that Sam had turned into this? At first it had seemed harmless enough, just a weird style phase. He had assured himself that wearing Goth clothing wasn't dangerous by itself. Now, however, the extremeness of her makeup and clothes had become a barometer of her emotional stability.

Alex opened his eyes. But what did he do with this?

"Daddy, are you coming?" Sam pointed to the seat across from her.

Trying to calm his mounting frustration, Alex forced on a smile and entered the nook, pausing to kiss the top of her head. He resisted the temptation to wipe his mouth, wondering what she could have put in her hair to make it like that.

"How did you sleep?" Alex asked, opening the fridge. He took out a carton of eggs and held them for her to see, his brows raised in query.

"I don't understand how you can eat the unborn." She shuddered and took another sip of her herbal tea. The haughty disdain reminded him of his ex-wife. Divorce certainly hadn't freed him of that.

"You ate them six months ago."

"I'm enlightened now." Sam heaved a sigh, tilting her head and putting on a martyred expression. Another perfect imitation of her mother.

If he could keep them apart, he might have a chance to help Sam. He had seen *Victoria* the week before. Now that she had a rich Frenchman for a husband, she was too good for simple "Vicki." Her thinness had surprised Alex, but Sam's recent odd eating choices had become clear.

Watching his daughter from the corner of his eye, he had to fight down feelings of loathing for her mother. Not for what the woman had done to him, though that had been bad enough. He didn't usually buy into the negative energy hate generated, but watching Sam slip through his fingers. . .

"Classes start next week." Alex scooped his scrambled eggs onto a plate. "Do you have all your books?"

Sam glared at him through hooded eyes.

"So, is that a yes?"

"Sure."

"Was there enough in your account, or do I need to transfer more money in?" Alex sat at the table and stabbed a forkful of eggs.

"I didn't look."

"Samantha!" He slammed the fork on the table and scrambled eggs flew across it. Sam squealed, pushing back and knocking the last of her tea into his plate. Breathing heavily, Alex stared at the mess.

"*You* did that." Sam shot him an accusatory glare. "No way am I cleaning that disgusting stuff up." She moved as though to slide past his chair.

"Stay here." Alex grabbed her wrist. It was so small in his hand, frail almost. A stab of fear went through him. Did she have an eating disorder?

"You're hurting me, Daddy." Sam's voice was small.

He let her go and looked at her, *really* looked at her, beyond the ghastly makeup and the disaffection. Where was Sam in there? With Vicki poisoning first her mind and now her body, was he going to lose his little girl?

"Baby, I'm sorry."

"Don't call me that." She rubbed her wrist, her mouth pouting.

"We talked about that school account. If you overdraw—"

"Fine. I'll look it up and tell you if I need more money in it." Sam stomped past him.

Alex grabbed a washcloth from the sink and went to work on the table. The college semester would start in a few

7

days. Thank heavens he would have that release. Otherwise, he might go crazy.

Francie stared at her reflection in the mirror. It hadn't been that hard getting used to Greg being gone, but Rafe's absence made the big old house seem so empty. Two months ago she had been cooking for three. Now, it was just her.

She picked up the curling iron and twisted a long strand of hair around it, considering the view of the large bedroom behind her. So many memories in this house. Good ones from when she was a child. Before Greg.

Not long after his first accident, only a couple of months after they were married, her grandmother had decided the old place was too much work and moved into a condo. Francie had been pregnant then, and Gran had insisted that she just needed someone to care for the place. In spite of the head injury, it had been something Greg could handle—until three years later, when a second car crash had put him in a wheelchair.

There was so much Francie would love to do to the graceful old house. Besides needing a new roof and fixing the dry rot along the eaves, it needed paint. Gran would die to see it now. She had worked hard to get it on Boone's official register of historic homes. It made Francie doubly sad that her beloved grandmother hadn't lived long enough to see her dream for the old place come true.

Francie turned and examined her hair. The dark strands flowed nicely down her back. In her other jobs, it hadn't been smart to look nice. Or pretty. Plain and drab meant fewer passes from creepy guys, either from the owners of the homes she cleaned or the customers at the Quick Mart.

She checked her mascara. The makeup had turned out well that morning. It was a good thing she had decided to practice Saturday. It had been so long since she had worn makeup that her first try had made her look like a student from the Mimi Bobeck School of Makeup Artistry. After practicing a couple of days, Francie had finally been happy with the results.

She tipped up her heel. The black pumps, though from Goodwill, were cute and almost new. They were the first heels she had worn in years, and she hadn't been able to resist the red sole. Especially after she had found the beautiful, secondhand suit with the red blouse. It was so classy, and the price so affordable, that Francie had kept looking over her shoulder, expecting someone to tell her there had been a mistake. Starting a new life, she wanted to try something different.

Stepping back from the mirror, she did a full figure check. She didn't recognize herself. How could a used outfit and some cheap makeup make her look so much younger?

Francie picked up the older model smart phone a friend had given her and activated the camera. Pointing it at the mirror, she snapped a selfie and sent it in a message to Rafe.

Look at the old girl now.

U better carry a gun with u Ma! Ethan asked if ur my sister. Haha

Francie already liked Rafe's Harvard roommate, Ethan, who had been present for the first online talk with her son. She had been worried Rafe might end up with someone from a rich family who had attended an Eastern prep school and would look down at a scholarship boy from North Carolina. But Ethan was from Montana and the stepson of a rancher. The young man's rough hands, tanned face, and sun-streaked sandy hair hinted at hard work.

haha

Good luck today, Ma.

<3

Francie was glad now she had agreed to let Rafe add her to his phone plan. Knowing she could text him made it seem like he wasn't so far away. She checked her purse again. The last thing she needed to do was forget something. Her first class was right after work. Grabbing the car keys, she hurried out the door.

The car wouldn't start.

Two

Alex got to his office more than an hour before his first class. He hadn't seen Sam yet that morning, so he was hoping she would show up looking like a normal Goth. He snorted. *Normal* Goth?

The first day of classes was always a little unsettling, but this year was worse. They had been hearing rumors for months that the department was doing something different with the administrative support, but the History Dean's office staff had been closed mouthed about it. Admin had better let the professors know soon. He already had plenty of work for his assistant—except he didn't have one yet.

Someone rapped on his door and opened it before Alex could say anything. Professor Kevin Eldred stood with his styled, graying hair, a plastic grin glistening with movie-star-white teeth. Whenever the guy turned on his smile, Alex expected a CGI light to sparkle on one of them. Kevin carried off casual professional easily in his suit and white shirt, minus a tie. The ladies loved him, but he always rubbed Alex wrong.

"Hey, Alex," Kevin said, walking in without an invitation and sitting in the cushy visitor's chair. He crossed a leg, spreading his arms out on each side. "Heard anything yet?"

"Nope." Alex moved to his desk and clicked on his computer.

"Why do they always give us old biddies? We need a little eye candy around here."

"Do you even know what that means?" Alex looked up.

"Sure. It means someone I could eat up."

"It also implies they're lacking in intelligence or depth." Alex typed in his password. "That might be fine for you, but I need a *working* assistant."

Kevin was about to say something when his phone signaled a message. While he dealt with it, Alex opened his email. There it was, a message from the Dean. A meeting with the new staff. Why were they waiting until the last minute? Irritated, Alex rose.

"Guess you got it too." Kevin got to his feet.

They walked together, Kevin blathering the whole time. Alex had never known a man before who could talk more than a woman. By the time they got to the conference room, Alex thought his blood pressure would have popped a blood pressure cuff. Never a good way to start a semester.

After shaking hands and greeting everyone, the Dean finally called the group to order.

"I'm sorry for the short notice. As you all know, the president has spent the last year looking at ways to lower the cost of an education here. You remember the time management study completed last year. This new program is what came from that. It will be a test for this school year. If things go well, we'll continue it in the future." He turned the time over to his assistant and left the room.

Over the years, Alex had experienced too many "head desk" moments with the college administration to have much confidence. Looking around the room, he realized he wasn't the only one who was concerned.

The Dean's assistant detailed a number of changes that Alex thought put a lot more work on the professors. He knew times were tough and hoped no programs were on the cutting block. The School of Business would be safe, for sure. Business, like sports, always seemed to have its "boosters." But history? Too often over the years, Alex had heard from many in the academic world that history was a fluff major. It was *art*, after all.

He was still trying to think through how differently he might have to work with his students and must have missed the assistant's last remark. The door opened, and a group of middle-aged women entered the room. Beside him, Kevin groaned.

"What?" Alex whispered, sitting up.

"Weren't you listening? *That's* our administrative support pool. And not a piece of candy among them." Kevin sat back in the chair, looking thoroughly disgusted.

"Why them?" No one looked familiar. Was the Dean not bringing back any of the previous year's staff?

"The school got a grant from the Feds. Women reentering the workforce or something. They get partial tuition for salary."

"Wait. Reentering the workforce?" Alex scanned the group, trying to see signs that any of them had skills. *"We're* supposed to train *them*?"

The assistant Dean spoke up, calling off the names of two or three professors then the name of a woman.

Alex's heart sank. Last year he'd had a great administrative assistant. Full-time, to himself. Now he was going to have to share the skills of one untrained person with another professor. Or two? Exhaling, he leaned back in his chair, awaiting his sentence.

"Our final administrative assistant, Francesca Davis, is running late this morning. She's assigned to Professors Eldred and Diederik."

The Dean's assistant left the conference room, and Kevin went off in a huff. Alex took his time standing and slowly made his way to the door. He listened carefully to the various side conversations, trying to get a feel for the caliber of the new assistants. Didn't he have enough on his plate right now?

Alex checked his watch and quickened his pace. Sam was supposed to meet him in his office before they both had classes.

She was waiting outside his door, looking almost normal in her dress and boots. All black, of course, even the lacy . . . thing around her throat. Alex wondered for the first time who was paying for her curious clothing. It better not be coming out of her school account.

"Hey, Daddy," Sam said, sliding her hand dreamily along the wall.

"Is that new?" Alex asked, unlocking the door.

"Yeah." She followed him inside and took the seat Kevin had used just half an hour ago.

"Did your mother buy it for you?" As soon as he said the words he knew he had made a mistake. Sam's whole body stiffened, and she glared at him with tight eyes. Anymore, he couldn't mention the woman without his daughter blowing up.

He hadn't even said anything about Vicki. Alex clenched his fists, trying to keep his anger under control. Why were they always trying to cast him as the bad guy? If Sam was spending his money, he had a right to know.

"No, my mother didn't buy it." Sam's voice had taken on a defiant tone.

"Did you use the book money I gave you?" Alex's voice rose. "And where are your books, by the way?"

"I'm going to get used books."

"Where are your brains? You know those go fastest."

"Where are my *brains*?" She jumped to her feet, all the lethargy gone. "First you attack my mother and then—"

"I didn't attack your mother—"

"Nothing I do is ever good enough for you!"

Sam wrenched open the door and stormed out of his office.

Francie was almost in tears by the time she reached the building. She had come to the campus over the weekend to get familiar with it, but she hadn't considered trying to find her way through a mass of busy new students—all while in a panic. *Late* on her first day. What if they fired her? Like being an administrative assistant for two professors wasn't terrifying enough. Why couldn't the federal program have been answering phones in the admissions office or something?

She looked at the piece of paper again for the room number. One floor up. Francie had just reached the elevator when the doors opened. A tall man in a suit bounded out, almost knocking her down.

"Whoa." He grabbed her before she fell, but he didn't release her. Instead, he held her out from him, eying her up and down. "Well, hello there, gorgeous." He gave her a flirty grin. "Why have we never met?"

Francie pulled away, her cheeks growing warm. With a wink, he let her go and jogged off. He made his way through the students, pausing to make what had to be teasing remarks, if she was reading his body language and the response of the girls right. Looked like some things never changed.

She pushed the elevator button again and started to wipe her palms on her skirt, but stopped. She didn't want to get anything else on her suit. The elevator doors opened, and Francie took a deep breath. Walking down the hall, she searched for the Dean's office. *Please don't let it be over before it begins.* She opened the door.

"Mrs. Davis?" asked a pleasant-looking man, who was talking with the receptionist.

"Yes, that's me. I'm *so* sorry—" Francie began.

"Don't worry about it. You called and let us know. Professor Eldred should already be in class, but you might be able to catch Professor Diederik before he leaves." The man gave her a room number and waved her off.

With a thrill that he hadn't fired her on the spot, Francie limped out the door. Why had she ever thought it a good idea to start wearing high heels again? *Today*? She found the office room number, confirmed by the name on the door, and was about to open it when she heard shouting inside. She stepped back just in time.

The door burst open and a pretty girl with long strawberry blond hair stomped out. Her headlong rush drove her right at Francie, who squeezed against the wall, almost out of the way. Their shoulders hit, and they both stumbled. As Francie steadied herself, she could see tears in the girl's heavily made up eyes. Staggering for a couple of paces, she managed to stay on her feet then ran down the hallway.

"Come back here," a man yelled from inside. He dashed out the door and halfway down the hall before it was obvious the student had made her escape.

Yelling at a student and chasing her down the hallway? *That can't be my new boss.* Francie couldn't help staring at the compact, but solidly built—almost buff—man, who stood with his back to her. The angry energy came off him in waves, and she had to fight a primal instinct to run and hide. Giving a quick glance over her shoulder, Francie began to edge away. Maybe she could pretend she hadn't seen. The man swore and spun around, seeming to see Francie for the first time.

"What are you doing there?" he growled. "Eavesdropping?"

"I, uh. No. I'm Francie Davis." Her stomach twisted painfully. She had given up her old life to go to school. If she lost this job, she would have to drop out.

"Who?" His tone made it sound like he thought she was an idiot to think he would know who Francie Davis was.

"I think I'm your new administrative assistant."

The man strode toward her then, fire in his dark eyes. "How *good* of you to *bother* showing up." His mouth turned up in a sneer, and he brushed past her.

Francie's face flamed hotter than when the other man had flirted with her. She began, "But I—"

"You were *needed* here an hour ago," the man interrupted, his tone now icy. "If you expect to keep this job, you'll have to learn the meaning of two things—*responsibility* and *dependability*. I have no use for a slacker." The professor grabbed a packet from just inside the door and turned as though to leave. He looked back and pointed to the inside of the office. "I have a folder on my desk. Let's see if you can follow simple directions."

Francie stood, shocked, until he had hurried down the hallway in the same direction as the fleeing student. With shaking hands, she stepped quietly into the office and closed the door. Sniffing, she put her purse on the floor by the front desk and went into the second office. She could hardly see as she lifted the single folder from the rigidly tidy desk. She took the folder to the outer office, sat down, and opened the file. A giant tear dropped, splattering his carefully written notes.

By the time Alex reached the outside of the building, there was no sign of Sam. What was wrong with him? He knew better than to play the heavy-handed card with her. The last thing he wanted her to do was to move in with her mother. Vicki had already said she and her new rich husband were planning a move to Europe and "what a wonderful opportunity it would be for Samantha." It would be, but not under her mother's questionable supervision. With Sam almost nineteen, if she decided to go with her mother, there was nothing he could do to stop her.

His anger had passed, and he couldn't believe he had just made a fool of himself in front of a total stranger. Alex glanced at his watch. The file he needed for his next class was in his office. Where that woman was. The memory of the hurt and confused look in her dark eyes made him cringe. After losing his temper twice in such a short time, did he dare face his new assistant again?

Feeling like an idiot, he hurried up the back stairs and slipped into the hallway. Alex peered around the corner just as the woman came out of his office, carrying the folder he had left for her to copy. He watched as she walked down the hallway, unable to ignore how well that black suit fit her. He straightened. That was not good. If she looked nice enough for him to notice, Kevin was sure to. Just what Alex needed, having Kevin's eye candy working for them.

When she disappeared around the corner, Alex dashed to his door and went inside. The Davis woman already had a couple of neat stacks on her desk. A picture of a good-looking young man in a cap and gown sat next to the phone. Alex scanned the rest of the desk. No photo of her with a husband or a boyfriend. Kevin would spot that right away.

It only took Alex a second to find the file. He listened at the door before opening and peeking around it. The hall was empty, so he jogged to the staircase, relieved that he had made it without seeing her. He took the stairs two at a time and blasted out the door, continuing to run. By the time he entered his classroom, he was breathing heavily.

"Hey, Professor D," a male student said from the second row. "Since you're late, does this mean we get a free ride the first time we're tardy?"

"You know . . . the rules, Reese." Smiling, Alex caught his breath and went directly to the front of the classroom. He put his folder on the table and faced the group. "*I'll* be in charge of the guillotine."

"Sick."

"Since a lot of your classmates seem a bit alarmed, Reese, why don't you explain the tardy rules?" Alex grinned when the young man jumped to his feet and hurried to the front of the room. With Reese in the class, this period was sure to be entertaining.

"See, if you're late you have to come up with a creative reason for your tardiness." Reese leaned forward, taking his time to scan the room and make eye contact with every student. "And not just *any* creative excuse." He straightened, pointing a finger toward Alex. "It has to fit the class material you missed because you're late."

Alex peered at him, his brows raised expectantly.

"Oh, yeah." Reese gave the rest of the class a conspiratorial wink. "Professor D will take note of anyone who's tardy. At the last class of each month, everyone with a mark will have to roleplay. "He," Reese said, pointing to Alex, "gets to choose our roles."

A girl on the front row raised a hand. Alex nodded for her to speak.

"What's with the guillotine?"

"Well, this *is* History 2100, Revolution in History. Thank you, Reese. You can take your seat." Alex picked up his marker and started writing on the whiteboard. "We will be examining the causes, character, and significance of political revolution in world history, concentrating on a major revolution of modern history. We'll consider why revolutions occur, who participates in them, and what effect they have." He turned to face the students. "If this isn't the class you thought you were taking, please drop it right away. There's a waiting list."

By the time the class was over, Alex felt much better. He erased the whiteboard, wondering why he had been so temperamental lately. If Sam had come to his office after this class and not before it, he was sure things would have ended differently.

Teaching, like that class, gave him a high, almost like when he ran. He loved finding ways to light the fire of interest in the eyes of his students. He wanted his classes to be memorable, something his students could look back on in years to come. For so many of them, history was a tough course. They had lived so little themselves it was hard for them to relate. Alex liked changing that, bringing the subject alive for them, and helping them to connect with the people of the past.

He was just closing his folder when he remembered the new assistant. His high disappeared. Alex really didn't want to face her again anytime soon. He glanced at his watch, feeling conflicted. She *had* been late which was unacceptable, but he should apologize to her. But if he apologized, would she think his apology excused her tardiness? Alex exhaled. Besides, he should probably talk to either her or Kevin right away. The other professor had to understand that Alex wouldn't put up with any shenanigans with the help.

As Alex climbed the back stairs again toward his office, he hadn't made up his mind whether he would try talking to Mrs. Davis or pull Kevin aside. Not that Kevin was noted for taking advice from anyone, and his mellow demeanor hid a nasty temper that Alex didn't feel like dealing with. He needed time to gather his thoughts before deciding how to approach her.

He peered around the corner again, struck by the ridiculousness of having to sneak around his floor. If the Dean saw him, Alex would look like an idiot. Of course, he would look like an idiot to anyone who noticed him.

His new assistant came around the corner from the copy room then, and he pulled back just enough to observe her. Maybe it wasn't a bad idea to skulk around after all. Except for the classroom, Alex struggled when he met people for the first time. Once he had a chance to get to know them, to trust them, he found it easier to open up.

As Mrs. Davis walked down the hall toward his office, she looked shorter than he remembered. A quick scan, ending at her bare feet, explained why. His lips twitched. She struggled a little with the copies as she unlocked his office door, and Alex almost went over to help her.

The memory of her hurt face flashed through his mind, and he hesitated. He really did need to apologize. To her and to Sam. But not yet. He used to be good at keeping his mouth shut when he was mad. Still fighting the residual anger from earlier, he knew that trying to talk to either of them now would be like stirring some dying, but still glowing, coals after a forest fire. He didn't want to spark anymore fights.

When Mrs. Davis disappeared into the office, Alex moved toward Kevin's door which was ajar, indicating the other professor was there. The new assistant came out again, and Alex pulled back. Then he heard Kevin's familiar, flirty voice.

"Well, well, well. So we meet again."

Alex surged to the corner, peering around it.

"Excuse me." Mrs. Davis tried to go around Kevin, but he stepped in her way.

"Hey, not so fast. You haven't told me your name yet."

"That's because you don't need my name." She tried to stand taller, but it didn't make much difference against the substantial height difference.

"But you're obviously an employee." He acted like he was going to point toward a small batch of papers in her arms but took one of her long curls in his fingers instead, twirling it around. "Are you new? Working for the Dean maybe?"

Alex was moving toward the pair before he gave it a thought. "Hi, Professor Eldred. Mrs. Davis."

Her back stiffened at the sound of Alex's voice. Was she more alarmed at him showing up than Kevin's obviously unwanted attention? Alex slowed his pace, stopping a couple of steps behind her.

"Oh, hey, Alex. I was just getting acquainted with this lovely lady." Kevin gave a conspiratorial grin, like Alex was in on it. "She's new here."

Pulling her head to the side and freeing her hair, Mrs. Davis turned to face Alex. Kevin shifted so he was at her side and even closer than when they had been facing each other. A frown crossed her face, and she edged away. Moving quickly, Alex squeezed between them, even though it placed them in an odd line, facing his office.

"Mrs. Davis, I see you've met Professor Eldred. He's the other professor you'll be working for." From the corner of his eye, he could see her blanch. "Have you finished my copying?" Alex gave her a subtle finger wave toward his office.

"I have it almost finished, sir. I'll put this on your desk right now." She hurried away.

"You've got to be kidding me," Kevin said, not waiting for her to get out of earshot. "*She's* our administrative assistant? I'm adding the Dean to my Christmas list."

The woman increased her pace, and Alex clenched his fists. She had to have heard that.

"I want me some of that," Kevin said just before she got through the door. A hint of a smile tugged at the corner of his mouth, and he seemed lost in his thoughts.

"Did you really just say that?" Alex hissed, giving the other man a not-so-gentle elbow to the ribs. After a football scandal over a decade before, the college scrupulously held annual mandatory sexual harassment training—in excruciating detail, in which one of the school's attorneys went over examples, lawsuit after lawsuit. After years of listening to those, no one could be stupid enough to do what Kevin had just done, not even Kevin. What was he playing at? "Did you hear me?" Alex asked.

"I was just kidding." Kevin finally looked at him, putting on his innocent expression.

For the third time that day, anger rushed through Alex. "You listen to me," he growled, spinning and pointing his finger in the man's face. Even though Alex was shorter by a few inches, he knew his time in the gym made him seem bigger than he was. Wiry Kevin stumbled back a step, his eyes wide with surprise. Alex said, "I don't want you upsetting our *shared* assistant. Call her Mrs. Davis. Did you hear that? *Mrs.* What if she heard what you just said? Do you want her husband coming after you?"

"You need to take a chill pill, man." Kevin straightened his jacket. "A guy can't even flirt with a pretty woman anymore." He shot one last glance at Alex's door and shrugged. "I've got a stack of things for *Mrs.* Davis to do too. I guess I'll go get them ready for her." He turned around, put his hands in his pockets, and walked toward his office. Whistling.

Alex shook his head. A confirmed bachelor, Kevin was forty-five—only a few years older than Alex—yet sometimes the man acted like he lived in the last century. This was the worst Alex had seen him. Was the guy going through middle-aged crazy or something? And it was only the first day of classes. Turning back toward his office, Alex paused and remembered his own interaction with Mrs. Davis. Was her husband going to come after him?

When he entered the office, she was quietly typing at her computer. He thought back to the sparse instructions he had given her and was surprised at how well she seemed to be functioning. Maybe this was going to work out all right after all.

"Do you need anything, Professor?" She was looking up at him.

Caught watching her, Alex felt like a fool. Where he had thought to apologize to her, the ice in her gaze killed all desire. "Let me know if you have any questions." He went into his office.

Once he saw Mrs. Davis's file, he realized why she had been placed with him and Kevin. Their schedules were complementary. Alex read that she was a recent widow, and her husband had died in June. And the first thing Alex had done was yell at her. Stellar. At least her husband wouldn't come after him.

Alex reviewed the rest of her information. Working full time *and* taking a full schedule of classes. His opinion of her went up. Good for her.

Now for Sam. Alex pulled out his cell phone and sent a quick text message.

Sorry I yelled at you.

I'm not talking to you

How many times had she said that? Sam was quick to blow up, but then it was over. Usually. Alex prayed this was one of those days.

What are you doing for lunch today?

You're dead to me

Alex groaned. She was really mad then. After nearly two years, he ought to know better than to mention Sam's mother in front of the girl. Early on, he hadn't been able to keep back his bitterness and hurt, even with simple things. Now, just mentioning Vicki brought Sam to her mother's defense, almost as though the girl expected him to say cutting remarks, and she meant to stop him. Alex should be a better father and not put her in that position. Leaning back in his chair, he wondered if Vicki badmouthed him in from of Sam. Did his daughter come to *his* defense? Did he deserve it?

It had been easier right after the divorce. Vicki had obviously been in the wrong. There was nothing like having sixteen-year-old Sam come upon her mother in a tête-à-tête to put the girl solidly on his side. Vicki had moved out a few days after Sam had tearfully called Alex to tell him what she had seen.

Lunch at 12:30? I'll buy you a salad.

No answer.

Be there or be square.

That usually got a response. Nothing. A rap on his door brought Alex to his feet.

"Come in." He put his cell phone on the desk.

Mrs. Davis stepped in and gave him a chilly look. "I'm sorry to bother you, sir. Do you need everything right away? Professor Eldred called to say he has some things he would like done before lunch. Since you have a class in fifteen minutes, I thought now would be a good time."

Wondering how many more women he could alienate in one day, he considered warning her about Kevin. The way she had moved away from Eldred showed she must have a measure of the man. She might be offended if Alex suggested she couldn't take care of it herself.

"That will be fine, Mrs. Davis." Alex picked up one of the folders she had made for him that morning. "Just so you know, starting next week, on Mondays I'll have meetings with the history club. We're cataloging potential new historical buildings this semester. I also have an open-door policy Monday through Thursday at three, but that doesn't start until next week. I need my assistant to be present when

I'm meeting one-on-one with students. Kevin, er, Professor Eldred has his student appointments on Tuesday and Thursday mornings, so there shouldn't be a conflict."

"Very good, sir. I'll be sure to make note of that." Mrs. Davis turned and stiffly walked away.

Alex followed the woman out the door, careful not to catch up with her. He felt an odd sense of sadness at her coldness, and he determined, at that moment, that he would get her to forgive him. Kill her with kindness, maybe.

Mrs. Davis had put her heels on again, and there was something endearing about the way she limped toward Kevin's office. That suit really did fit her well. Not that he was looking.

Three

Francie woke up early Saturday morning to catch up on the garden. Boone's Blue Ridge Mountain weather was more like New England than the rest of the South, so she had a shorter growing season. With her books costing more than she had expected, she would be relying even more on her bottled food to get her through the winter. The price of college textbooks was nothing short of a racket.

As she made her way down one of the long garden rows, the cell phone she had in her pocket went off. Recognizing the ring, she hurriedly wiped off her dirty hands on her ratty jeans so she could accept the call.

"Rafe, you're up early this morning. I thought a college student like you would have been up late on a Friday night."

"Well, you know." Rafe sounded tired.

"Don't listen to him, Mrs. D," shouted Rafe's Montana roommate from the background. "He hasn't been to bed yet."

"Rafe!" Francie paused and rubbed her temple with the back of her hand. "What are you thinking?" She had always been glad Rafe had never been drawn to the party scene in high school, dedicating himself—as she had—to getting the Harvard scholarship. Was he going to blow it all with his first shot at full freedom?

"Shut up, Ethan." Rafe's voice sounded like he was walking, and a door clicked. "Don't worry, Ma. We went to a frat party, and I volunteered to be on the Sober Crew. Ethan and I are checking out the fraternities to see if we're interested in rushing any of them—not that any of the rich kids are likely to look at me. Ethan's step-family has some connections, so he's got a better chance of getting in. It's still a good way to meet people."

"Did you?" Francie took a deep breath and bent over to pull a weed. She should have known Rafe better. He was a man now, but there was still enough of the boy to resent her interference.

"Meet some new people? A few, but I'm not sure any of them will remember either of us. So, tell me about your week and the new job."

Francie wondered what to tell Rafe—not about being yelled at by Professor Diederik. At least she didn't appear to be at much risk of him firing her anymore. If anything, the guy seemed to be going out of his way to be nice to her. She definitely didn't want to tell Rafe about creepy Professor Eldred, who now barely spoke to her.

"Everything is just so different from how I imagined it nineteen years ago."

"How about your classes?"

"I was scared to death until my only in-person class had a student in it with white hair." Francie laughed. "I'm glad it's nothing like high school. Every teacher I've talked to has been understanding. I've already had to email a couple of them. Good thing I have easy classes."

An image came to mind of the handsome Professor Diederik sitting in his office, wearing dark, horn-rimmed glasses for reading. Since Francie had seen his schedule of classes, she knew if she had taken American History that semester, he would have been her instructor. It made her shiver a little. Was he a tyrant in the classroom like he had been to her that first day, or the nice but reserved man he had been since?

When he wasn't yelling at her, he was really quite an attractive man. Dark hair slightly peppered with gray, and an almost military cut around the ears and neck. The longer front that he seemed to like combed back sometimes flopped charmingly down his forehead. She liked it better than the way Professor Eldred wore his hair, which was longish and almost scruffy looking. Francie also liked the way Professor Diederik was clean shaven while Professor Eldred liked the two-day-old, not-quite-a-beard look.

"You sound like you're outside. Weeding already?"

"Yes." She pulled herself out of her reverie about Professor Diederik. Why was she wasting her precious free time thinking about him anyway? It was hard enough staying mad at him when he was being so nice. "I'm going to work on my homework later, while the jars are in the water bath. But tell me about your classes."

By the time she hung up, Francie had finished weeding and had filled a decent-sized basket. With Gran's equipment, she and Rafe had been able to maintain the large garden by themselves. Alone, Francie was finding it a lot harder to keep up. She picked up the basket.

Stopping, she shifted the heavy load to her hip and turned to stare at the neat, colorful rows—ripe purple eggplants, red tomatoes, the deep blues and reds of the berry bushes, the herb garden that kept going to seed. She would have to prime the okra again which was nearly done with its season.

For a moment, it all overwhelmed her. There was too much to do. How could she work, and go to class, and do homework, and freeze and can food for the winter all by herself? What if she didn't put up enough food to last her? Francie took a deep breath. No need to panic. It wasn't like she had to feed an active, hungry teen-aged boy anymore. She only had herself to worry about.

When had she come to rely on Rafe so much? She missed him, missed him coming into her bedroom after a date and telling her all about it, missed watching him play sports and going to his band concerts, how he would see her working on something and jump up to help, the way he had taken to jumping to her defense when Greg would say something horrible.

What if Rafe didn't come home next summer? His roommate might get him a summer job at that ranch in Montana. Rafe would see it as the great adventure it was. He would jump at the chance . . . or would he? Francie thought back to the conversation in the graveyard and his offer to stay in Boone. She couldn't let him pass up opportunities because of her. It was time she got used to being an empty nester.

She glanced around the garden again. Her practiced eye told her there was no way she could put it all up before the food went bad, but she would have plenty to share with the local food bank.

Somewhat mollified, Francie took off her shoes at the door and headed for the large kitchen where she had the canning supplies out already. Rafe had wanted to plant hot peppers that year for the first time. She had found a yummy looking salsa recipe online she meant to try, and Rafe could tell her if it was any good when he was home for Thanksgiving.

Alex lifted his eyes from the book, tilting his head to hear better. He glanced at the clock. Nearly midnight. Sam had been true to her words all week, treating him like he was dead. Not wanting to fight with her again, he had played along. She usually came around when he did that.

Not this time. When he got home on Friday, she had packed the bag she took to her mother's. A quick check of her bathroom had assured him she had only packed the things she usually took for a weekend visit. What had she been doing there? Partying with her mother's new, rich friends?

The old clock in the hallway that had belonged to his grandmother rang midnight. His condo was off the beaten track; he usually liked the quiet little place he had purchased after the divorce. Now, it seemed oppressive. Was this what his future held, living alone here?

The sound of a familiar engine purred up the street and into the parking lot outside. Alex let out his breath, relief flooding him. Sam's car door slammed shut. Lifting the book from his lap, he tried to appear engrossed in it. He needed to find a hobby, so he could pretend to have a life.

On the porch, Sam fumbled with her keys, grumbling. Before he could get up to unlock the door for her, it burst open, blowing a furious, swearing Sam inside. She stopped when she saw him and stared for a moment, her eye sockets blackened with the worst of her Goth looks. So it had been a bad day with her mother too. Through the makeup, her eyes glistened, and black rivulets ran down her cheeks.

As Alex stood and tossed aside the book, he wondered if she was going to scream at him again. He didn't say anything but held out his arms to her, as he had so many times when she was growing up. She wanted to come to him; he could see it in her eyes where several emotions did battle.

He didn't move, and she finally threw herself into his embrace, sobbing as though her world had come to an end. What could have happened to upset her so badly? It took all his willpower not to ask her. *Sam's an adult. I have to respect that.* He said it over and over in his mind until his daughter's thin body stopped shaking. Then he guided Sam to the couch and sat beside her, keeping an arm around her shoulders.

"Ah, baby—" he began then swore. "Sorry. I know you don't want me to call you that anymore."

Sam giggled and looked at him, sniffing. "You make me laugh when you curse. It's so not like you."

Alex reached over to the table, picked up a box of tissues, and handed them to her. While she wiped at the makeup—it was a hopeless case—he pressed his lips tight to keep from questioning her. She finally gave up on her face and looked at him.

"Daddy, I'm sick and tired of having to defend you and Mom from each other."

"I'm sorry, baby—" He grimaced, and she giggled again.

"It's okay. You can call me that." She patted his cheek, giving him a what-do-you-do-with-the-old-man eye roll that she hadn't used since Before.

Alex heaved a sigh. Anymore, everything was either Before or After her mother had left. He wanted desperately to get back the Before Sam.

"I'm sorry," Alex began again. "What's between your mother and me should stay between the two of us. It's not fair to you. I know your mother loves you."

Sam leaned over and laid her head on his lap, stretching out her legs on the couch like she used to do when she was younger. Alex swallowed the sudden lump in his throat and reached for the remote. Mystery Science Theater 3000 reruns were always good for a late-night laugh. His ex-wife had never understood his and Sam's obsession with MST3. Vicki had never made an effort to.

Alex tried to remember when Vicki had changed. She had always been fascinated with status and money. He had been too stunned at his good luck that someone like her—beautiful, chic, sophisticated—would consider the grandson of poor immigrant Germans to give any thought to her ambitions. He was young and in love. They had never talked about what they wanted out of their life together.

While he went through college, Vicki had been supportive and encouraging, working full time right up to the day she went into labor with Sam. Two weeks later, she had taken their tiny daughter to work with her. Thinking back, Alex was sure that, even back then, Vicki's goal had been for him to be a university president. Too bad she hadn't asked him what he wanted.

While his daughter chuckled at the ridiculous old science fiction movie and the host's commentary, Alex worked hard to keep his breathing steady. What was his ex-wife saying about him? Whatever it was must be pretty bad for Sam to come home so upset.

He forced his hand to unclench and used it to gently stroke Sam's long hair. The tightness in her shoulders relaxed, and it wasn't very long before her breathing slowed. Careful not to disturb her, he raised his feet to the ottoman and pulled a throw from the back of the couch, tossing it over her.

Leaning back his head, Alex closed his eyes. If he was going to yell at anyone, it was Vicki. But not where Sam could hear.

Four

It was nearly three weeks before Alex got the call he had been waiting for, longer than usual. His ex-wife could only go so long before she had to get her "dis Alex fix." He had gotten through the first year after the divorce thinking that he would have less contact with Vicki once Sam had turned eighteen. Not so. His daughter might have become an adult, but sometimes it seemed that all he had to do was *think* about his ex, and she would call in all her snarky splendor.

He was glad Mrs. Davis was still away from her desk, so he wouldn't have to hold back. He still hadn't been able to bring himself to apologize to her. She continued to look at him like he was a cell under a microscope. Or maybe something to be dissected—or vivisected. It did serve him right, but how long was the woman going to stay mad at him?

Alex clicked the speaker button on his phone and leaned back in his chair. He was determined not to lose the upper hand in this conversation.

"Hello, Vicki."

"I told you not to call me that."

"It was good enough for seventeen years."

"I merely put up with it for all those years."

Alex could imagine how she must be tilting her nose in the air. He usually replaced the image with one of a turkey looking up in a rainstorm and drowning in its stupidity.

"What do you want to talk about, *Victoria*?"

"The only thing I would make any call to *you* about. My daughter."

"*Our* daughter."

"Whatever."

"Sam was pretty upset when she came home a few weeks ago."

"You know how emotional she is. She'll get over it."

An image of Sam's tear-stained face went through Alex's mind, and he clenched his fists, fighting against an adrenaline rush. When Vicki blew off their daughter like that, he always got angry. When he got mad, he didn't show up well, and Vicki knew it.

"Have you made up your mind about Samantha's study abroad next semester?"

"I'm still talking about what happened to upset Sam." He winced at the edge in his voice and took a deep breath.

"There's nothing to talk about."

"Badmouth me all you want." Alex was pleased at his level voice. "But save it for when Sam's not with you. It's not fair to her."

"Don't tell me what's fair to my daughter. She has to see you as you really are and not be blinded by her childish devotion. I don't want her to make the same mistake I did."

Childish devotion? Heat flushed through him, and he wiped his top lip. Yes, Sam was immature for her age and had been since the day she had caught her mother in bed with a man other than Alex. He had often wondered if his daughter's retreat into immaturity had been an unconscious attempt to restore her stolen innocence.

But he wasn't going to remind Vicki of that. The woman wasn't sorry about her infidelity. The one time he had brought it up, she had launched into him with a long list of his sexual failings. Alex felt a little sick. Vicki couldn't be sharing her thoughts on that with Sam. *Please.* He took a deep breath.

"Anything in particular about me you were picking apart this time?"

"The list is *so* long." Vicki let out an exaggerated sigh. "That weekend I told Sam I didn't want her saddled with a man like you, who has no ambition. You've wasted your life teaching history—*history, Alexis!*—in a podunk town in an insignificant state. I tried to guide you, but like most men with small ideas you wouldn't have it."

The old argument always made his pulse quicken, and he didn't try to lower his voice this time. They had argued about this again and again through the years they had been married. He wanted to teach, not administer programs. When had Vicki become this vicious woman?

"Stop it, Vicki! Stop pitting Sam between us."

"Oh, now you're yelling at me." Her voice came out a satisfied purr. "I hope Samantha is there to see this nasty side to your personality. I could tell her all about the violence."

"*Violence?* What are you talking about?" Alex sputtered.

"Oh, I could tell her all about the times you wanted to hit me. I could see it in your face. She needs to know how much you frightened me, how it drove me into the arms of another man. Yes, thank you for reminding me. I think our next mother-daughter chat should include a little discussion about violent men. Now, enough about *you*, Alexis. I want to know what you've decided about Samantha studying abroad next semester."

"I told you already." Weary, Alex let Vicki change the topic.

"Samantha says she won't go unless you give your blessing. Why are you taking so long to decide? Alexis, we have discussed how important it is for her to be exposed to the European culture."

"No, *we* didn't *discuss* any such thing. You told me I was paying for her to go on study abroad. I told you Sam had mentioned it to me."

Alex hated the thought of vulnerable Sam being gone so long and under her mother's less-than-tender care. Vicki's husband had a bad reputation for holding wild parties. During the summer, Alex was sure he had seen a picture of his ex-wife in a Paris newspaper at a party where a lot of people had been arrested and where there had been accusations of the presence of underage drinking and date rape drugs.

"You're a pathetic excuse for a father. You've never loved her," Vicki said, her tone taking on an essence that always made him feel like someone had poured acid down his throat, and it was burning its way to his heart. "Depriving your daughter just so you can feed your ego."

Alex clenched his jaw while she ranted on. *She's goading you. Don't fall for it.* If he lost control, he would gain nothing, and he didn't want to get pulled into playing her games again. He clung to the thought that Sam had said she wouldn't go without his blessing.

"Vicki," he said, when she seemed to be running out of steam. She went off again, so he raised his voice. "*Vicki.*"

"I'm done talking to you, Alexis."

"What did I do that made you hate me so much?"

She paused. "You stopped being a man." The phone went dead.

Francie put the earphones in her ears with shaking hands. She really hadn't meant to eavesdrop. If she had realized Professor Diederik was having a private conversation, she would have slipped back out of the office.

He must have been so engrossed in that awful phone call not to have heard her return. The conversation had drawn her right in, and she had forgotten she shouldn't be listening to it.

Now that he had hung up, Francie typed furiously, hoping to look busy and not guilty. When he didn't come out, she pulled the headset from her ears. The door was open, but she couldn't hear anything from the room.

"Stopped being a man." What an emasculating thing for that shrew to have said. Francie couldn't understand why she felt so defensive of the poor man. After all, he was the one who had yelled at her and said such insulting things. He probably deserved—

Francie leaned back in her chair. No, she didn't believe he had deserved those horrible words. She hadn't wanted to admit it, but she was sure Professor Diederik had been about to apologize to her a couple of times. And she had cut him cold. Ashamed of herself, Francie wondered if she was no better than that . . . *woman*. No better than Greg. Francie felt a little sick.

Putting in the earphones again, she went back to work. A few minutes later, she sensed more than saw the professor come out of his office and pause. Francie kept working, pretending she didn't know he was there.

"Mrs. Davis?" His voice was tentative.

She didn't answer, just plucked away at the keyboard, hoping he wouldn't notice the trembling of her hands. If she looked at him, would he be able to tell she had overheard?

"*Mrs. Davis.*" Professor Diederik's voice was louder then.

Francie steeled her expression and turned in her chair. "Oh, Professor. Are you off to class now? I'll have this finished before you get back, so I'll just go take care of Professor Eldred's work when I'm done."

"Good plan."

Watching him leave almost hurt. Everything about his posture as he walked down the hall spoke of defeat. Had Professor Diederik been on the phone with that witch just before the incident with the student the first day of school, when he had snapped at Francie? She was pretty sure she would strike out at people after talking to the woman.

Was the professor's ex-wife like Greg had been, making snide, cutting remarks—little jabs that could just as easily have been done with a knife? And left as many scars? Greg had always apologized later, promising he hadn't meant to hurt her.

Every year he had gotten worse, shouting about how stupid and lazy and ugly she was. If he hadn't been saddled with her, he could have done something with his life. Francie had believed it. That was why her parents had thrown her away at eighteen, why Greg couldn't find anything good about her. *She* was the problem.

Then he had started in on Rafe. Beaten down, Francie could believe she was stupid and inadequate, but her perfect little son wasn't. And she wouldn't sit back and let Greg say those awful things to a child.

She glanced toward the professor's open office door. That awful woman. And they had a daughter? Francie shivered and turned back to her work. She couldn't let him know she had overheard, but she wanted to do something to cheer him up.

After putting paper in the printer, Francie pulled her purse out from under the desk. For lunch, she had brought a small jar of a new preserve she had made. Rafe had named the original version Cheberry Preserves, a blend of strawberries, raspberries, and cherries. With this batch, she had added a hint of jalapeño, to what she thought was great effect. She was sure Rafe would love it and hoped the professor did too.

So many times over the years, especially after Greg had

had a bad day, she would have appreciated a gesture of kindness from someone. Anyone. Francie polished the little jar with her blouse and went into Professor Diederik's office. Not wanting to spy, she didn't look around but placed the preserves in the middle of the desk so he would be sure to see it first thing.

Feeling better than she had since she had begun the job, Francie finished her morning work and headed to the Central Dining Hall where she hoped to get ahead on her assigned reading while she ate lunch. Her stomach was rumbling by the time she found a little table tucked away in a corner. She sat with her back to the wall.

One thing she loved was being able to get a good view of the college environment. She still didn't feel a part of it, but she loved being around people, especially those who were actively engaged in learning. The place was bustling with people. Francie wasn't surprised when a girl carrying a tray approached the table.

"I can't find a seat anywhere else. Can I share your table?" The strawberry blond girl didn't wait for an answer but slid her tray on the table, pushing Francie's book against her lunch bag. The girl pulled a phone from her backpack and started typing on it.

Recognizing her, Francie closed the book, deciding this might be more entertaining. She wished she dared ask the girl what she had been fighting with Professor Diederik about on the first day of school. Her makeup had been quite heavy but was lighter now, showing what a pretty girl she was. Her startling green eyes had been masked by the heavy eyeliner and mascara before. Was she wearing contacts?

The girl looked up from her phone. "You keep looking at me. Do I have something on my face?"

"No." Not sure how to take the girl's attitude, Francie opened her brown paper bag and pulled out a veggie sandwich on homemade bread.

41

"Are you for real?"

"I'm not sure what you mean," Francie said, trying not to be offended. She was used to being complimented on her cooking. Even Greg hadn't been able to find anything wrong with that.

The girl pointed at the sandwich Francie had pulled from the plastic wrapping. "You're really bringing food from home?"

"I don't have money for eating out." Francie hated the flush she could feel creeping up her neck.

"What, you spend all your money on your clothes?"

Francie glanced down at the suit she had bought for her first day. It was only the second time she had worn it. She decided to address the girl's remark the same way she had when Rafe used to get snarky with her.

"I like you." Francie picked up half of the sandwich. "You remind me of when I was young and rude. What's your name?" She took a bite of her lunch.

The girl blinked then giggled. "All right. I deserved that." She reached out her hand in a very formal gesture. "You can call me Rose."

Taking time to wipe her fingers on a napkin, Francie reached across the table and shook the girl's hand.

"You can call me Francie."

"Francie? Like fancy but with an "r" in it? That's kind of cool. Is that short for something?"

"Francesca. It's a good Italian name, and my parents didn't want me to forget my heritage."

"Mine's short for Rosamunde." Rose said, pulling the plastic lid off her salad. "Your parents sound a little like my grandmother. She's my dad's mom and came here from Germany. It was all drama because of the Berlin Wall. I guess they had to sneak out of the country or something. You know, that whole crazy *Sound of Music* kind of thing, where they had to hide while people were hunting for them. I don't personally believe it." She stabbed a section of lettuce and daintily dipped it into what had to be a fat-free dressing.

Francie swallowed before speaking. "That kind of thing really used to happen. I had a friend in elementary school who had to sneak out with her family. I found out about it when she came to a sleepover. We were about ten, and she woke up with a really horrible nightmare. It was scary. Her mom had to come and take her home because she was too freaked out to stay the rest of the night. She kept talking about people chasing them with guns. Is your grandmother still alive?"

"Yeah." Rose played with her salad. "So you don't think she's making it up?"

"I don't know anything about your grandmother. Is she honest about other things?"

"Uh, *yeah*. She's my dad's mom. They're all totally rigid with the truth. Now, if it was my mom's mom . . ." Rose rolled her eyes.

"I've got some relatives like that. If I believed everything my mother's first cousin said, she should have written a book, a tell-it-all about the scores of Hollywood movie stars she was supposed to have dated."

Rose giggled again. "My other grandmother's like that." She stopped laughing, and her face became serious. "My mother is too."

"I'm sorry. That can be really awkward. I can't tell you how many times I wanted to laugh in my cousin's face. What was weird was she really seemed to believe what she was telling us. I don't know if she lives in a fantasy world or maybe has a mental disorder. She's never hurt anybody with her make-believe stories, but it's still kind of pathetic."

"Some people do it to hurt, though." Rose looked sad, as though she spoke from experience.

"Would you like some homemade bread? It's good, even if I say so myself."

43

Rose considered the slice of bread Francie slid toward her.

"Have you ever had homemade?"

"My dad's grandmother used to make it before she died." She shrugged. "It was okay."

"You don't have to eat the whole thing. I wish I could offer you some homemade preserves to go with it, but I gave the jar away this morning. They were *so* good!" Francie leaned forward, conspiratorially, and Rose did the same. "I put hot peppers in it. Just a little."

The girl straightened and gave Francie a curious look. "You made it yourself? Like the bread?"

"I told you. I'm poor. I grow most of what I eat, especially now that I'm in school."

"Wow. I've always wanted to learn how to cook."

"Your mother hasn't taught you?" It was Francie's turn to shoot Rose an inquisitive glance.

"My mother's more into the professional, pay-someone-else-to-do-it thing. At least for as long as I can remember."

"I'm doing up another batch Friday night." Francie folded her paper bag so she could use it again. "I have to get the fruit done before it goes bad."

Rose's eyes widened. "Um, are you inviting me over to watch?"

"Hon, if you come, I'll need you to do more than watch. If I had someone to help me, I could get it all done and not have to worry about it anymore."

"You live alone?"

"I do now my son's at college. He used to help me."

Rose hesitated a moment more. "I'd like to come and help you. Should I bring an apron?"

"I've got plenty of those. I'll even feed you dinner, if you don't mind not having meat. I can't afford it."

"I don't eat meat." Rose shuddered.

They exchanged phone numbers, and Francie texted her the address. "I don't get home until about five. It's outside of town."

"Does everyone have their assignments? For you new club members, don't forget this is just the initial contact with the homeowners." Alex glanced around the small group. They fit easily in the conference room which made him frown. Until last year, his Historical Architecture Club had needed to meet in one of the small classrooms. Several of the older members had graduated last summer, but this big a drop meant he would need to shake up how he was doing things to get more students interested.

"Professor D?" Amy, directly across from him at the table, wriggled her arm enthusiastically.

"Yes." Alex bit back a smile at her gesture.

"Isn't this new one out off of Old Bristol Road?"

He reached for her list, and she handed it to him. "It is. Too far for your clunker?"

Amy nodded, but he could tell she was using her car as an excuse. How did these kids think they could get on in a business environment or, heaven help them, as parents if they had to have someone else do everything for them?

"I remember this one," Alex said. "The phone number's been changed. It's definitely going to need a personal visit, so I'll take it, but I won't be able to get out there until Saturday." He shot her a glance that made it clear he was on to her.

She gave him a sheepish look and ducked her head.

"Any other questions?" When no one else spoke up, Alex dismissed them and gathered his papers. He didn't mind going out to the old house. Since it was on the outskirts of town, it might take a little convincing before the property owners were willing to let them all come in and catalog the place. He wished he could take Sam with him.

As Alex returned to his office, he thought about his conversation with Vicki. Unless he was willing to go down to her level, he could never win against her attacks. He just wouldn't do it, but there had to be a way to protect himself if she was going to start throwing out ridiculous accusations.

Mrs. Davis was gone when he got back to the office. He paused at his door, staring at the jar on the desk. It was a canning jar, the small gift size his grandmother had made for neighbors during the holidays. Curious, he sat in his chair and picked it up. He unscrewed the cap and tapped the lid. It wasn't a frozen jam then. Something had been written in a neat hand on the top with a permanent marker. *Cheberry.*

Alex took his letter opener and pressed it against the seal. It gave a satisfactory pop, and he knew it hadn't been opened since it had been canned. Sniffing, he inhaled a luscious bouquet of fruits that made his stomach growl. Berry, he assumed, but something else. He held it up to the light, but it wasn't translucent like jelly. He thought he could see round fruits in the purplish substance.

He put the jar on his desk. There weren't any students out to poison him that he knew of. The fruity aroma made his mouth water. He loved berry jam—or preserves. Alex ran a cautious finger lightly over the top and touched it to his tongue. Sweetness flooded his mouth, followed by a little kick. Intrigued, he opened his drawer and grabbed a fast-food packet with a knife, fork, spoon, and a napkin. With the spoon, he scooped some out and slid it onto his tongue, savoring the taste like a wine taster with an expensive vintage.

A groan of pleasure escaped. Alex picked up the cap and read the words again. *Cheberry.* What an inadequate name. Whoever had been kind enough to leave the jar—one of his students?—was his new best friend. With a smile, he took another spoonful.

Five

fter work on Friday, Francie hurried into the house to put the casserole in the oven and change her clothes. She wasn't convinced Rose would come, but she wanted to be prepared if the girl did. The night before, Francie had taken the time to set up the kitchen. It wouldn't be wasted time, even if Rose didn't show up.

Francie was just walking down the stairs, pulling her hair back in a ponytail, when she heard the car outside. She stopped to blink back surprise tears. Except for the mailman on Saturdays, she hadn't heard a car drive up to her house since Rafe had left.

She hurried to the screen door and opened it with a grin. Rose was getting out of a little Accord, her head tilted back to take in the house. She turned to Francie and mouthed 'wow.'

"It's old and falling apart," Francie said. "Keep your shoes on right now. We need to pick the fruit first."

Rose's jaw dropped. "We're going to pick the fruit too?"

"The fresher the better, my grandmother always said."

Francie slipped her shoes back on and led Rose across the large porch that nearly circled the house. At the kitchen door in the back, she reached in and pulled out two aprons. Armed with clippers and two baskets, Francie took her helper out to the garden.

"You did this all by yourself?" Rose stepped to the end so she could see up the various rows.

"Rafe—he's my son—helped me put it in last spring, and we maintained it over the summer. I've only had to do it alone since he left for school."

"You live here alone?" Rose shook her head. "Doesn't it scare you being out here by yourself? Do you have a dog?"

"We never had one because my late husband was allergic to them. He died last June," Francie added before the girl could ask. "Now, let's show you what to do."

By the time they carried their full baskets into the large kitchen, the sun was starting to go down. They put the baskets on the table.

"Something sure smells good."

"That's dinner. Should be ready to eat in a while."

"I never knew berries had so many stickers." Rose went to the sink and washed blood off her hands.

"I *did* offer you gloves." Francie pulled off hers. "I probably should have fed you before I put you to work."

"After all those berries I ate, I don't think you need to worry about starving me."

They set to work, and Francie was pleasantly surprised at what a good student Rose was. Inexperienced to anything but kitchen basics, yes, but she wasn't afraid to step right up and do something new.

"We'll do them in smaller batches." Francie poured the three cups of sugar into the pot Rose stirred. Francie glanced back at the bag of sugar. She ought to have enough to last the canning season, then it would be gone. Maybe she could get a temporary job for the holiday break. She had money enough only for her utilities and keeping her car running. At least until she got her grants for the new semester. She groaned.

"What's wrong?" Rose peered at her, concerned.

"Oh. I was just wondering what I'm going to feed my boy when he comes for Thanksgiving."

"Big appetite?" Rose laughed. "My dad's an old man, but he works out, and he really chows it down after a workout." The smile left her face. "It used to bug my mother."

"It doesn't anymore?"

"They're divorced. And not amicably."

Francie gave the girl a quick hug. "I'm sorry." She turned up the heat for the water bath, careful not to look at Rose who sniffed.

With the last batch in the pot, they sat at the large, worn, old table. Rose stretched out her legs, working her feet back and forth.

"My gran used to say her 'dogs were barking' when her feet hurt." Francie pulled the casserole dish from the oven. Rose limped over to take a large potholder from the counter. She put it on the table, and Francie set the dish on it. Both of them inhaled deeply, the savory smell of roasted eggplant, tomatoes, and onions making Francie's mouth water.

"That smells so good." Rose hurried and grabbed forks.

Francie dished out their servings, and the two women ate in tired silence.

"Can I have some more?" Rose looked unsure, and Francie remembered telling her about being poor.

"Eat up. They're calling for a freeze this weekend. Anything left on the vines will die."

When the entire casserole dish was empty, they looked at it and then at each other, laughing.

"This was fun, Rose. Thank you for helping out. How many jars would you like to take as your pay for tonight's work?"

"I can't take your food." The girl's eyes went wide. "You need it to live on."

"I can't eat all those jars of preserves. Please, take a couple of them."

"All right. I'd better get going. I didn't realize it was so late." All at once, Rose threw her arms around Francie and squeezed her tight. "This is the most fun I've had in like . . . *forever*."

"I enjoyed it too." Francie blinked several times, overwhelmed by the girl's demonstration. "Now, be careful. I feel bad sending you home so late. There's not much traffic out this way this time of night. Use your brights until you get to town."

"I will, and thanks for the preserves. I think my dad might like these." She stepped into her shoes on the front porch then turned back. "If you need any help, will you call me?"

"Are you sure?"

Rose gave an enthusiastic nod, her eyes almost pleading.

"I'll be up early in the morning to go at it again, but I have to be done by noon to study." She wondered how such a sweet girl could be so starved for attention.

"I'll come. What time?"

"I'll be out in the garden at seven."

"I'd better hurry home then, so I can get some sleep. Night." She skipped down the stairs and to her car, waving again before pulling away.

Francie waited until the taillights were out of sight. Turning, she looked at the large entryway. The whole house seemed to echo with its emptiness. How could the presence of one lonely, painfully thin girl change the atmosphere of the old place so much?

Alex looked up from the book in his lap, tilting his head to hear better. He glanced at the clock. It was like a repeat of that awful weekend when Sam had come home crying. This was supposed to be *his* time with her. Had she gone out with friends? With a guy? He remembered the fun group of kids she had run with before the divorce and wondered where they were now. Some of them must be attending ASU. Had she connected with some of them again?

The sound of an approaching car made him pause and listen. The high-pitched whine told him it wasn't Sam's. What would he do when she finally did move out on her own, maybe even far away? He rubbed his eyes. Was he part of Sam's problems? Was she not getting past the divorce because he was still in limbo himself?

Alex rose from the recliner and went to his computer desk. Maybe he should check out some of those dating forums. He opened a browser and typed in "online dating." Scrolling down the list, he frowned. *FrenchKiss*? *HookingItUp*? Were these dating sites or escort services?

He continued down the page until he found one that looked legitimate. It required him to register and create a profile. Reading a little further, he realized the profile was essentially an ad to sell himself. Thinking back on Vicki's comments, he wondered what he could say that would be both honest and appealing to a woman. He couldn't think of one thing.

The sound of Sam's car speeding into her parking stall and screeching to a stop announced her arrival. Alex leaned back in his chair and waited. It wasn't long before Sam burst through the door as she had before, but this time she was practically dancing. She paused only a second.

"Oh, Daddy. I just had the most fun!" She skipped over to him and sat on his lap. Throwing her arms around his neck, Sam gave him a big hug. It was the tightest hug he could remember getting from her for a long time.

"What did you do tonight? Go out with friends?"

Sam stood and did a little pirouette. "No, I met this older lady at lunch. She's so poor she has to grow and cook all her own food. I think she even has to reuse the brown bag she had for her lunch."

"Uh, they call that recycling, Sam." Alex imagined an ancient, white-haired dowager, with purple-veined, arthritis-crippled hands, carefully folding a wrinkled, grease-stained sack.

"Oh, shut up. It's different when you *have* to do it."

She flopped backward on the couch, throwing her arms behind her head like she was lying in a meadow and gazing at drifting clouds. Whoever the ancient one was, he could tell she had made an impression on his daughter.

"So what does this have to do with where you were tonight?"

Sam turned her head toward him. "We got to talking, and somehow I found out she was going to be making jam. You know I've always wanted to learn to cook. I asked if I could help her." She shrugged. "That's what I did tonight. See this?" She got up from the couch and showed him the cuts and scratches on her arms and hands.

"Didn't she have any gloves you could use?" Alex scowled.

"I wanted to have the experience, to see what it was like in the olden days when people had to work the land."

Sam took up a pose worthy of an old-fashioned melodrama heroine in the summer plays, and Alex coughed to cover a laugh. Sam's obvious enjoyment of the day made him happy. He hoped the old woman knew what she had done for the strange child-adult she had opened her home to.

"I heard that laugh." Sam pointed a finger at him. "What have you been doing? Please don't tell me you've been sitting in that old chair waiting for me."

"I did read for a while," Alex confessed before pointing to his screen.

She came to stand behind him and looked at the monitor. "Are you kidding me? Online dating? That's brilliant. Why didn't you do this sooner?" She didn't give him a chance to speak but pushed him out of his chair and sat in it herself. "Let me help. This will be fun!"

Alex bent over her shoulder to see what she was typing. "Hey, wait a minute. *Ripped*? Samantha Rosamunde Diederik. Don't you dare write that. I don't want to meet some woman and have her find out that everything she thinks she knows about me is a lie."

"Oh, please, Daddy. You might not be tall, but you have a six-pack. And don't forget your *guns*."

"My *what*?"

"Your biceps. You are *so* twentieth century."

Alex shifted uneasily as she kept typing.

Donna K. Weaver

Six

On Monday, Francie slid into her work desk and turned on her computer. Rose had been a no show. Until receiving the girl's text near noon on Saturday, apologizing for oversleeping, Francie hadn't realized how much she had been looking forward to talking to the girl again. Rose had sent a second text explaining that her father wanted to take her to a matinee.

Francie stood and stretched to reach a binder above her desk. The door opened behind her and, from his pleasant aftershave, she knew it was Professor Diederik without seeing him.

"Good morning, Professor." She turned, pulling the binder to her chest. "Did you have a good weekend?" She thought he looked better, but there was still a wounded shadow in the back of his eyes. At least that woman was an *ex*-wife. Francie knew too well what it was like to dread going home.

"Uh . . ." He paused, giving her a curious look, like he wasn't sure what she meant. "Yes, I did. You?"

"Busy." Francie handed him a post-it note. "I'm off to the copy room. You've had two messages so far this morning." She slid past him and out the door, humming.

As she was going past Professor Eldred's office on the way back from the copier room, she thought she saw Rose going into his office suite. Francie paused outside. He wasn't scheduled for student appointments in the morning and never on Mondays. Uneasy, she wasn't sure what to do. Professor Diederik would never schedule an appointment with a student unless he knew Francie could be there.

With a sigh, Francie sat at her work station in Eldred's suite. She wasn't supposed to be there for another hour and a half, but she couldn't leave the girl in there. Francie leaned back in her chair so she could hear better. Just low voices. Keeping one ear tuned to the office, she went through the paperwork she would be working on later in the morning.

The door opened, and Francie spun around in her chair. Rose looked at her from the opening, Professor Eldred behind her. He scowled at seeing Francie, but Rose grinned. She looked so different from the first time Francie had seen her.

"Hey, Francie. Do you have an appointment with Professor Eldred too?"

"No, I work for him." Francie shot him a hard look. "I'm sorry, sir. I thought your student appointments were Tuesday and Thursday mornings. I would have made sure to be here if I'd known you needed me."

Rose's fair cheeks darkened, and she looked guilty. "I'm going to be late. Thanks a lot, Professor." She hurried out the door.

"Sir, I seem to have forgotten the university policy," Francie said when the girl was out of sight. "Can you help me remember?"

"That idiotic—"

"It's not idiotic, sir. My doctor always has a nurse in the room during annual examinations. It's as much for his protection as it is for mine."

56

His expression changed from irritated to angry. "I don't need another lecture." He went into his office and slammed the door.

Troubled, Francie headed back to the other office. *Another* lecture? What was he talking about? When she got out to the hallway, Professor Diederik was just coming out of his suite door.

"There you are. I wondered what happened to you."

"Sorry." She hurried her pace. "Professor Eldred had a female student in his office. I had to wait outside."

"Idiot." Professor Diederik frowned, looking down the hall.

"My thoughts exactly."

"Mrs. Davis—"

"Can I ask a favor?" she interrupted, stopping in front of him.

"What do you need?"

"Can you call me Francie? Every time you call me Mrs. Davis, I think of my mother-in-law." She dropped her gaze. "I don't mean to speak ill of the dead, but she was a very unpleasant woman."

"Sure. I can call you Francie. That's an unusual name. I don't think I've ever known anyone else with it."

"It was my great grandmother's name. It's short for Francesca." She glanced at him, surprised to see he was smiling. It accented the crow's feet around his eyes. For the first time, Francie noticed the wrinkles around his mouth, happy wrinkles she always called them. Even though he had never smiled at her before, she could tell he must do it a lot to leave permanent creases like that.

"It's pretty." He shoved his hands in his pockets, his expression turning serious. "I can't call you Francie unless you call me Alex."

"Alex. Is that short for Alexander?"

"Alexis. Like yours, it's an old family name."

"Alexis," she repeated, rolling the word over her tongue.

"Only my ex-wife calls me Alexis anymore and only when she wants to take a jab at me, so please call me *Alex*." The corners of his mouth twitched. "Or I'll call *you* Mrs. Davis."

"Alex for sure, then." Francie wondered why calling him Alexis would be a jab.

He stood watching her, his cheeks spread in a smile, and the shadow that had been lurking in the back of his eyes disappeared. Had her anger and coldness to him been a part of that? Well, not anymore. Francie smiled back, as warmly as she could, happy that her boss wasn't an ogre after all. Alex coughed and went into his office.

Back in his office to get what he needed for his next class, Alex paused. Mrs. Davis—Francie—was humming. The tune was soothing, and he decided she probably had a pleasant alto voice when she sang. Her smile came to mind.

Stepping back so he could see where she sat, Alex watched Francie work. What had happened to make her so happy the last couple of days? Had she met someone? An unusual sensation swept him, and he frowned. Why would it rub him wrong that she might be seeing someone? He didn't care.

She pulled out a drawer, revealing bright folders, obviously color coded. The anal organizer in him wanted to check out her system. Alex nodded. That was it. He didn't like the idea of her seeing someone because, if she got all loopy over a man, it would impact her productivity.

"Do you need something, Alex?"

She watched him expectantly with her bright, happy eyes. Where they had once been cold, they were now dark and expressive. Rich and deep. He blinked, confused.

"No, I, uh," Alex stuttered. "I forgot something."

He fled back into his office and grabbed his jacket. What was *that* all about? Alex didn't look at her as he hurried out the door. He was in bad shape if a pretty woman's pleasant manner was enough to mess with his head like that. Maybe it was a good thing he had let Sam write that dating profile for him.

Outside, Alex shivered and turned up his collar against the cold, late September wind. The trees in the foothills were already changing color. It was going to be an early winter. Few people realized that hot and muggy North Carolina had sections with a cold climate. It might be one of the state's best-kept secrets. Opening the folder, he tried to distract himself by flipping through the tests he would be returning in the next class.

Alex almost ran into someone and had to close the file for everyone's safety. At once, Francie's dark eyes and beautiful smile came to mind. He shook his head and started to jog. If he got to class a little early, he might have time to check the email Sam had set up for the online dating account. If he could remember the password.

There were already a few students in the classroom. All of them had questions which kept him busy right up to the start of class. After back-to-back classes, Alex was ready for lunch, so he headed over to the Central Dining Hall. He grabbed a burger and sat near a window where he had good reception.

It took three tries, but he finally got into the new email account. He leaned back in his chair. A dozen emails? The first two were instructional ones from the site, so he moved to the next one. Holding his sandwich in his left hand, Alex clicked open the first email from someone called *IAmUrDestiny*. He groaned. Not that he could say anything. Sam had chosen *KnightWeight* for his user name.

"*KnightWeight*?" he had asked.

"Sure. Don't you get it? Knight is for history, and Weight says you're a lifter."

"No, I think it says I'm an idiot to do this."

"Daddy! Work with me on this." Sam had giggled and nudged him with her elbow, giving him a sly look. "And Knight hints at being a hero without being in your face about it. Because you are, you know, to me."

With the lump in his throat, Alex hadn't been able to argue anymore. So his dignity had been sacrificed on the altar of fatherly love. If his baby was willing to forget their recent arguments, he would do just about anything for her.

Reading through *Destiny*'s email, he wondered what Sam had written in his profile. Stupid of him not to have looked. How much fun had she had at his expense?

By the time Alex finished his lunch, he had deleted seven of the emails. He sent tentative responses to the other three women. Peering more closely at one of their pictures, he noticed a billboard in the background for a movie that had come out at least ten years earlier. The woman in the picture looked forty, so she must be fifty now. What age had Sam put on his account?

He was throwing away his garbage from lunch when his phone dinged receipt of an email. Did he really want to see who it was from? Alex reached into his pocket. Sam would ask him at dinner, so he had better look. It was from *Destiny*. She wondered if he would like to meet. That seemed really fast. What did he do now?

By Thursday, Francie and Rose had eaten lunch together every day. Francie wanted to ask the girl about her meeting with Professor Eldred, but none of their topics had come close enough to make a natural transition. Maybe if she came over again on Friday night, they could talk about it.

"What are you up to this weekend?" Francie carefully folded the paper bag. One more time, and she could throw it away.

"Ugh." Rose rolled her eyes. "I had to promise my mother I would stay the night with her on Friday. She's such a drama queen." The girl scrunched her face. "I am too, sometimes. This summer I thought if I tried to be like her maybe she would let up on me and my dad. She married this creepy guy from France, and she's moving there in January. Mom wants me to live with her."

Francie considered her response, trying not to show her alarm. It seemed that almost every new revelation about Rose's life added to Francie's unease about the girl's situation. It was obvious she was keeping a lot back. A mother who was never satisfied with her daughter was bad enough, but a creepy stepfather too? Francie had learned the hard way to pay attention when her instincts said a guy was creepy. She took a deep breath, trying to calm down her desire to bring Rose home with her where Francie could keep her safe.

"What's it like at your mother's? Does she do fun things?"

"They're really into parties. Mom likes the French approach to underage drinking." Rose scowled and leaned closer. "I swear Michel's tried to get me drunk a couple of times, whenever his friends are there." She shuddered then blushed. "I didn't mean to say anything about that."

"Does your mother know about this?" Francie reached across the table and laid her hand on Rose's.

The girl shook her head, her expression closed off. She sat stiffly in the chair, almost daring Francie to ask any more questions. She had a strong feeling that if she did, Rose would leave, so Francie put her folded brown bag in her purse.

"It's supposed to freeze tomorrow night." Rose handed back Francie's empty plastic container. "Do you need help tonight bringing in the rest of your stuff? I can come over after school. You keep bringing me these yummy foods. I feel like I need to pay you back."

"You can come over any time you want, and not because you need to pay me back. I don't know how to cook small, and my son's not there to eat the leftovers. You're doing me a favor."

"If you're sure." Rose stood and picked up her backpack. "I have to get to class."

"Rose."

The girl turn back, her expression guarded.

"Listen to your instincts." Francie clenched her fists and tried to push away the ugly memories. "I used to clean houses. Early on, I didn't listen to mine, and a guy tried to rape me." She brushed at her eyes. He had threatened to press charges against *her* for assault when she'd hit him in the head with a lamp to get him off her. Since it was a situation of her word against his, her boss had fired her.

Rose's face softened, and she whispered, "I will." She started to turn but looked back. "Is five okay? I can start picking if you're not home yet."

"That'll be great."

Rose was already busy in the garden when Francie got home. Throwing on some jeans and a sweater, she dashed outside. The wind was picking up, and she wondered if it might freeze sooner than forecasted.

By the time they had lost the light, their baskets were full. Shivering, they hurried into the warm kitchen and washed up. Francie watched with satisfaction as Rose went right to work, remembering every detail from Friday. While the girl worked, Francie got dinner out of the fridge.

"Sorry you have to eat this twice today." She tilted the casserole dish so Rose could see the contents, before sliding it into the oven.

"Why don't you just nuke it?"

"Foods lose their crunchiness in the microwave. This dish is still good cold, but not soggy."

When they had finished washing all the fruits and vegetables and stowing them in the large, old refrigerator, dinner was ready. Francie put the steaming dish in the middle of the table, while Rose got the plates. She leaned over it and took a whiff.

"All this summer while I was trying to be like my mother, I was starving myself so I could get super skinny like she is." Rose scooped out a huge helping of crispy vegetables and cheese. "If I keep eating your cooking, Francie, I won't fit all those tiny clothes she bought me."

"Do you mind gaining weight? You're awfully thin."

"If I get to eat like this every day, I don't care if I weigh two hundred pounds." Rose took a bite and chewed, practically humming with pleasure. "Besides, I've felt better all this week than I have in months. I like eating like this. When I was hungry all the time, I got so depressed. I'm not sure I could go back to that. I want to try some of your recipes on my dad. Do you dry all your spices? Will the ones we have at home taste as good as yours?"

"I just dry the standard stuff and buy the exotic ones, like cinnamon. How did your dad like the jam?"

"Oh, no!" Sam put her hands to her mouth and giggled. "I totally forgot. When I got home I helped him sign up at an online dating site. The next morning I was in a hurry and pulled them out and forgot about them. I don't even remember where I put them. If find them, I can use them for dessert with my special dinner. I wish I didn't have to go to my mother's tomorrow."

"Why do you have to go? You're over eighteen."

"You don't know my mother. The price is too high to pay if I don't make a showing. Choose a recipe you think I can handle, and I'll fix it for him on Sunday."

The wind gusted and rattled the screen door. Francie

and Sam ran to look out the window. In the light of the back porch, huge drops of rain had begun marking the dirt outside.

"Oh, honey. You'd better hurry home before it gets any worse."

"Yeah." Rose threw on her coat and grabbed her bag. "Can you send me the recipe?"

"Of course. Text me when you get home."

"Okay."

Once again, with Rose gone, the house seemed to close in on Francie. She watched from the front window until the car's rear lights faded. Another gust of wind made the windows rattle, and a squarish object flew down from the roof.

"No, no, no!" Francie jerked open the door and dashed out front. Whatever had come down was long gone. She faced the house, lifting a hand to block the porch light. The wind blasted her, and she stumbled. Another piece of the roof came flying off, and she scrambled to catch it before it blew away. The brittle shingle was split nearly in half and came apart in her hands.

A large rain drop hit her cheek, and she brushed it away, but it was followed by another and then another. A flash of lightning lit up the sky, and a couple more shingles flew off. Would she still have a roof when the storm was over? The rain hit like someone had poured a bucket of water over her, and she darted under the shelter of the large porch.

How could she pay for a roof patch? What if the whole thing had to be replaced? Granny Gladys had trusted Francie with her home. The old woman would hate to see how it was falling apart. The wind shifted, and the stinging rain drove Francie into the house.

With a huge sigh, she went to the kitchen to get some pots. She hoped she could find all the leaks.

Seven

lex checked the address for the historical house again. He hadn't been out that way in years. Driving down the road, the bright Saturday morning sunshine made the clean air sparkle. After the freakishly cold storm on Thursday night, it had taken most of the afternoon on Friday before the ice melted. While still chilly, the day promised to be beautiful.

The sudden drop in temperature had made the trees change colors practically overnight. The crisp, bright reds, golds, and oranges of the leaves made him smile. Fall had always been his favorite season, and the changing colors were one of the reasons. He wished Sam hadn't had to go to her mother's. It would've been a beautiful day to take a hike. Maybe Sunday.

Alex saw the corner of the building, the roof hidden behind bright yellow leaves. His pulse sped up as he turned into the drive, and he got a full view. What a great old house. With the feel of an old farmhouse, it was surrounded by a covered porch that, even in this cold weather, seemed to invite him to pull up a rocker to sit and enjoy the scenery.

He parked the car and got out, turning so he could see the same view as the people in the house. It was far enough from town to give any visitor looking for peace and quiet exactly that. Taking his time, Alex walked around the front, examining the status of the upkeep. The place was shabby, but not crumbling. A fresh coat of paint would fix a lot, though it looked like there were some shingles missing, maybe from the storm the other night.

The porch was even better looking than it had been from the street. The owners had a quirky assortment of old chairs that added to the charm of the place. He stepped onto the doormat and stomped his feet as he knocked. At first, he didn't hear anything, but then a sharp rap rang out like someone hitting wood with a hammer.

Alex moved back onto the sidewalk. The noise came again, this time obviously from above. The owner must be fixing the roof. He walked toward the back where the sound was coming from. A figure in a red knit cap and a heavy coat raised an arm.

"Hello there," Alex called.

The person jumped and turned toward him. "Alex?" the familiar voice said. Then she lost her balance, sliding off the steep roof with a scream.

He ran forward, reaching out his arms as if he could do something from where he stood below. For a second she clawed at the eaves of the roof, but her grip failed. She hit the porch's roof with an awful crunch and a cry of pain, before tumbling off the edge. Alex lunged to catch her, but her heavy boots hit him square on the chest, and they both went down.

It took a second before Alex could catch his breath. He put his arms around the moaning woman on top of him. When he was able to speak, he tapped her red cap. "Francie, are you all right?"

She lifted her head and looked at him, tears running down her bright red cheeks. "Ow. Ow, ow," she gasped. "Are you hurt?"

"I don't think so. Can you move?" She nodded, and he gave her a soft push. As she moved over to her back, she cried out in pain.

Alex rolled to his side. "Where does it hurt?"

"My ankle."

He got to his knees and rubbed his chest. That was going to leave a mark. He scooted down to her feet, and he could tell immediately by the way she was holding it which one she had hurt. After he unlaced the boot, he pulled it off as gently as possible, but she still cried out.

"Sorry, sorry." It was already swelling and showed signs of bruising. Alex's stomach turned; he was responsible for this. "I have to get you inside, so we can put some ice on this. And I'll drive you to the hospital. They should x-ray it to see if you've broken anything. Are you hurt anywhere else?"

"I don't know; I hurt everywhere. There's ice in the freezer. Alex, I can't go to the hospital. I don't have insurance." Francie rolled to her side, moaning as she moved the foot.

"What are you doing?" Alex put his hand on her hip and rolled her to her back.

"I have to get into the house."

"Let me help you." He stood, wondering how best to get her upright without jarring the ankle. He bent over her, moving his hands first to put them under her arms, then shifting them to her hands then back to her arms.

Francie choked back a laugh, and Alex relaxed. "Is there anyone else here who could help me?"

"No one close. I live alone."

"I don't think I'll have a problem carrying you inside."

Her already flushed cheeks seemed to go a little redder, and she struggled to sit up. Alex stepped behind her and put his hands under her arms. She stumbled and fell back against him. He put his arms around her waist to keep her from falling again. How had he never noticed how good she smelled, like fresh air and sweet summer days and comfort food?

"Can you hold yourself up on your good foot? You do have a good foot, don't you?" He let her go, keeping one hand on each elbow to steady her.

"I think so." Her breathing was ragged, and her hands shook a little.

He stepped to her side and moved to put an arm behind her legs. "I'll carry you inside."

"No." She hopped away from him and turned to face him, wincing with the movement. Her eyes were wide.

"You can't walk in by yourself," Alex said, frustrated. "Just that little movement hurt you, didn't it?"

She stiffened her chin.

"Fine then. I'll do something else." He turned his back to her and backed up until he was right up against her. She had to put her arms around his waist to keep from falling over. Before she could say anything, he reached back and grabbed a leg with each hand, squatted down, and hefted her onto his back.

Squealing in surprise, Francie threw her right hand over his shoulder and down his chest, clasping her hands together. He carried her to the front door and turned so she could reach the handle. She opened the screen door, and he used his foot to push it more open, before repeating the process with the front door. He paused in the spacious entryway, Francie still on his back, and looked around.

"This is a wonderful old house. How many bedrooms are there?"

"Um, Alex, can you put me down?"

"Oh, sorry. Where's the kitchen?" She pointed the way, and Alex carried her into the large, comfy room and put her on a chair. He dashed back to the living room and grabbed a cushion from the sofa. Once he had settled it under her foot, he went to the freezer. He stared at the old-fashioned plastic ice trays. He hadn't known they even still made them.

"There are zippered bags in the drawer, there." Francie waved a finger at a bank of drawers. "Second one from the top."

Alex twisted the ice tray, unloading the cubes into the bag. He added a little water before closing the seal. With a folded towel, he set it gently on her swelling ankle.

"It doesn't hurt as bad now," Francie said after a few seconds. She looked at him. "Why are you here, Alex?"

"I didn't know this was yours." Alex pulled a piece of paper from his jacket pocket and handed it to her. "The house was recently added to Boone's list of historical homes. Each year, my Historical Architecture Group selects a handful of homes to catalog for the state. I volunteered to check out this one. I'm really sorry about making you fall. Do you have any painkillers I can get for you?"

"Above the sink, up high."

"Where are your glasses?" She pointed again, and Alex opened the cupboard above the dishwasher. Right where he would have put them. Without thinking, he opened a couple of other doors and smiled. Her spices were in alphabetical order, just like his. Aware of the silence, Alex turned around to find her watching him.

"Did you find what you're looking for?" Francie seemed amused. Her red cap was askew, and strands of her long dark hair feathered out.

"Sorry." He retrieved the glass and medicine and handed them to her. "I'm not usually nosy. I was just admiring how orderly your cupboards are. My daughter would tell me that makes me a total geek."

"I don't have time to be disorganized. I held down two full time jobs until I came to work for you, and now I have classes and homework." She sighed. "I don't have time for a sprained ankle either. I was going to can most of the weekend, after I fixed the roof."

"Don't worry about the roof. I can take care of it for you." When she looked about to argue with him, Alex distracted her by lifting the bag of ice and the towel to check the bruising. "How does it feel?"

"Better." Francie shifted the foot cautiously, wincing only when she turned it to the side. The toenails were painted bright red.

"Did you leave the hammer on the roof? I don't remember it following you down."

"I don't honestly remember." She gave an embarrassed laugh. "I hate to think what that must have looked like."

"You scared me to death." Alex put a hand on her shoulder and squatted down so they were eye level. "Seriously, I thought you were going to die."

"Thanks to you, I didn't." She reached across and touched his shirt. "Do you need an icepack too?"

"I'll be fine."

"Prove it." Francie crossed her arms, her face set with a stubborn look.

Alex almost ignored her, but her expression reminded him of the face his mother had worn when he was a boy and pretending not to be hurt. He finally shrugged off his jacket and undid the top buttons of his shirt.

Francie gasped, and he looked down. Yes, a definite mark. He could make out most of the outline of her boot heel on his right pec. Flexing the muscles, Alex hissed, surprised he hadn't noticed it sooner. He lifted his right arm and rubbed at the tender, swollen red mark. Hammering would probably work out some of it.

"You *do* need some ice."

"I'll be fine." He buttoned his shirt and put his coat back on. "Let me shift you to the couch where you'll be more comfortable."

"You're hurt. I wish you wouldn't go on the roof."

"Will you let me take you to the hospital to have that ankle x-rayed?"

"No."

Alex shrugged, wincing only a little. "Then I'll patch your roof."

She glared at him for a moment before throwing up her hands. "Fine. Fix it, then. But I'm not sitting on the couch while you do it. Bring me that desk chair. It has wheels."

"What are you going to do?"

"Cook."

Alex hesitated for a second before doing as instructed. Helping her into the chair, he said, "You have to keep that foot up."

Pinching her lips, Francie grabbed her leg at the knee and put it over the chair arm. "There."

"That's not high enough to keep the swelling down. Kind of defeats the purpose."

"So I'll only put it there when I have to get something. When I'm at the table, I'll rest it on the chair."

"Stubborn woman."

"Stubborn man."

"I'll go find that hammer." Alex grinned, liking her spunk.

He went out the back door, and Francie used her good foot to scoot the chair to the window. Alex Diederik was going to fix her roof. As he scouted around the yard for the missing hammer, he kept rubbing his chest. She *knew* it had hurt more than he'd admitted. *And heavens, his chest.* Francie fanned herself absently and tried to ignore the throbbing in her ankle—and the too-attractive man wandering outside her house.

She collected the vegetables she would need and brought them to the table. When she had everything in place and was able to lift the injured foot to the chair across from her, Francie sighed with relief. How was she going to get around campus if she couldn't walk?

Alex must have found the hammer because pounding began overhead. How much was that aggravating his bruise? She didn't care what he said; his chest needed ice too.

When the casserole was ready, Francie hooked her leg over the chair's arm and picked up the dish. Staring at the too-tall oven, she sighed. She opened the oven door and slid the casserole dish inside. Francie moved her leg off the arm then used the counter to pull herself to her good foot, so she could turn on the oven. Not wanting to do all that again, she hopped to the fridge to see if there was another tray of ice.

She was still at the freezer when she heard Alex on the back porch. At the sound of him stomping his feet on the mat outside her door, Francie's breathing quickened. *Stop being a fool; he's your boss.* The door burst open.

"What do you think you're doing?" Alex was behind her, pulling her hands back from the freezer faster than she would have dreamed possible.

"I'm getting ice."

"Let me do that after I wash my hands." He brought over the desk chair and helped her back into it. "What smells so good?" He sniffed the air, the gesture reminding her of Rose.

"Your lunch." Francie held her wrists against her chest and found herself watching him, looking so comfortable and at home in her kitchen, as he washed his hands then filled another bag with ice cubes. When he brought it to her, she said, "That one's for your chest."

"I'm fine. How's your ankle?" He removed the towel and ice. "Can you move it?"

Francie did carefully and bit back a groan when she turned it to the side.

"That's enough." Alex put the fresh bag of ice on her ankle then put the first one in the freezer. "You have any rubbing alcohol? If you add a little to the water it won't freeze completely. Makes it more comfortable against the swelling."

"I might have some in my emergency kit, but that's upstairs."

With a shrug, he came to the table, pulled back a chair, and twisted it so he could sit on it backward. "What are you working on there?"

"I'm getting these ready to can. I don't know what to do now, since I had to use all my big pots in the attic when the roof started to leak."

"I can fetch them for you." Alex stood again. "Just point me in the right direction."

"You mean up?" Francie laughed at his expression and told him where to find the door. She continued to cut up vegetables, listening to the comforting sound of another person in the house.

It took two trips, but Alex brought back all her pots. He put them on the counter and turned on the tap.

"You had to haul all of these upstairs by yourself?"

"Who else would do it?"

"Okay. I understand that." Alex looked over his shoulder. "Is that a picture of your son at the top of the stairs?" When she nodded, he said, "He's a good-looking kid. You must miss him. My daughter is thinking about going on a study abroad next semester. I hate to think what it would be like with her gone."

"Well, *this* is what it's like," Francie said, irritated at the burning in her eyes. "Rafe's at Harvard, and I haven't seen him for six weeks. It's the longest we've ever been apart and talking on the Internet just isn't the same thing."

"A Harvard man, huh? Good for him. That takes a lot of work." Alex turned around and grabbed a towel to dry off the pot. "For both of you." He looked around the kitchen. "Even more so if he's there on scholarship."

Francie considered Alex for a moment, trying to take the compliment and not be offended by the assumption. It was true and stupid of her to be prideful over such a thing. She kept chopping.

"Please tell me," he said, standing by the stove, "that whatever is making that heavenly smell is almost done."

Right then the timer at Francie's side went off. They both jumped, and he went straight to the drawer with the potholders as though he already knew where they were. She made room on the table for the plates he handed her. Like he was the host and she his guest, Alex placed the steaming casserole dish on the table between them.

He served her first, even though she could tell he was anxious to taste it. Francie held her breath when he blew on a forkful and put it in his mouth. With closed eyes, he chewed slowly, but his expression didn't change. Having always been delighted when people liked her cooking, her heart sank at the delay in response, and she prepared herself for the tactful but disappointed comment.

Opening his eyes a little, he let out a deep breath. "Ambrosia," he finally said and took another bite. Francie let out a shaky laugh, picked up her fork, and tried not to grin too broadly. When Alex had taken a few bites, he started picking through his plate as though looking for something.

"No meat," she said. "But I grew everything else. I even made the cheese."

"Is there anything you can't do?"

"Be on time for the most important job I've ever had."

Alex said something under his breath that she thought might have been a curse. "Francie, I've wanted to apologize since I said that. I'm sorry."

"Thank you."

"Now I see your situation, I feel even worse. I'll bet you were worried I'd fire you."

"Well, for the first few days, yes, but you were always nice after that, so it was hard to stay really mad at you." She put another scoop of casserole on his plate, and he picked up his fork again.

"You were such an ice queen." Alex chuckled. "Every time I thought I could bring it up, you'd give me that look. You scared me to death."

Francie gave him a look she had always used on Rafe, when he was exaggerating.

"See." Alex pointed his fork at her. "There it is."

"You're funning me."

"I'm not." Alex became thoughtful as he chewed. He finally said, "I'll bet Sam would like this. She's my daughter, and six months ago, she turned vegetarian.

"I can give you the recipe. Just yesterday I shared it with Rose—she's a cute kid I've kind of adopted. I can't believe so many kids don't know how to cook. Rafe was in the kitchen with me by the time he was five." She didn't mention that it had been as much to avoid his father as to learn.

"I'm glad you've had some help around here." He pushed away his empty plate and stood. "Now, what can I do to help you?"

"You don't have to—"

"I know that." Alex crossed his arms, wincing once and loosening them a little. "But seriously, I don't have anything else to do today, and I feel responsible for your ankle. Let me help you."

"Fine, then."

Alex started clearing the table. When she tried to scoot herself over to help, he held up both hands. "No offense, but you'll be underfoot with that thing."

"I have to wash my hands again before I work with the food."

"All right. Do that while I put this in a container."

Francie took her time at the sink, only partly because it was awkward to reach with the desk chair turned sideways. When she finished, he handed her a towel and rolled the chair back to the table. As she watched him puttering around her kitchen, she remembered how her grandfather had done the same thing. Granny Gladys had mentioned several times that it had taken her a while to find Grampa, but he had been worth the wait.

That evening, after they had eaten dinner, Francie finally let Alex help her onto the couch in the living room. She couldn't believe what an efficient pair they had made. Next week it would be easy to can what was left.

"This is the best food I've eaten in years." Alex dropped beside her and propped his feet next to hers on the ottoman. "Where did you learn to cook?"

"Granny Gladys taught me. She and Grampa talked for years about turning this place into a bed and breakfast. He died three months after he retired. That was about the time my husband was first injured. I was pregnant with Rafe and sicker than a dog. When we got married right out of high school, my parents disowned me."

"You mean they literally disowned you?" He reached over and squeezed her hand.

"Yes, but it wasn't about money because they weren't rich. It was about 'making my bed and lying in it,' according to my father. I was overwhelmed. We'd only been married six months, and I was already behind in rent. Our landlord was getting ready to evict us. Then Gran showed up at the apartment, telling me this place was too much for her, and she didn't have the heart to do a B&B anymore. She didn't want to sell the place either since her grandfather had built it."

"Why did she think you could handle it by yourself, especially being pregnant?" Alex still held her hand in his. Almost absently, he started running his thumb back and forth over the top of it.

"Until Greg's second accident, he was able to work the place."

"When was that?" Alex asked, his voice soft.

Francie looked up from their hands. Alex slid his head

closer, and her breath caught. "We'd been married almost three years," she managed to get out.

"So you've been taking care of all of this for . . . ?"

"Sixteen years."

"You're an amazing woman, Francie Davis," Alex said, his voice a little husky. His eyes dropped to her mouth for a second, and he slid his head closer still.

"Would you like some bread and jam?" she asked, before he did something he might regret.

Her question seemed to wake up Alex, and he sat up, releasing her hand. "Sure. Tell me where it is, and I'll get it." Alex jumped to his feet.

"In the pantry. The really small jars."

Francie used the time to get her breath back and hoped her wits would follow soon. She was sure he had been about to kiss her. Why had she stopped him?

"It was *you*," Alex shouted from the kitchen. He appeared in the doorway and held up a small jar of Cheberry Preserves, the one she and Rose had made the other night.

"I thought you knew that."

Alex shook his head, returning to the couch with the little jar in hand. "I get stuff from my students all the time. Sometimes they're just being nice while other times it's bribery." He sat beside her again and used the edge of a spoon to pop the seal. After handing her the top, he scooped out a blob and put it in his mouth.

Francie burst out laughing, pleased, but a little appalled too. "Didn't your mother teach you any manners?"

"Not when it comes to this stuff. I ate that whole jar in one sitting. Cheberry. What kind of name is that?" He took another bite.

"Rafe came up with it. It was getting late in the strawberry season, the cherries were on, and so were the blackberries. He said we ought to make them into a jam. We liked it so much it became a family tradition. This summer, when we put in the garden, Rafe wanted to try jalapeños. I ended up with so many, I wasn't sure what to do with the extras. I decided to try a little bit in the Cheberry recipe."

"So that's what's giving it the kick. I love it," Alex mumbled, keeping the mouthful of preserves on his tongue longer.

"What's your story, Alex?" When he almost choked, she quickly added, "Since we're sharing."

"Vicki and I were never really good together, even at the beginning." He put the jar and spoon on the end table, leaned back on the couch, and put his feet up on the ottoman, his hand finding hers again. "Vicki always wanted more than I did."

"More stuff?"

"More everything," Alex said, lacing his fingers through hers. "More money, more status, more promotions. I tried going after the kinds of things she wanted, but I didn't care about that stuff. My heart wasn't in it, so nothing I did was ever enough. I will give her credit for *one* thing—besides Sam. If not for Vicki, I wouldn't have gone after my Masters, and I'd have been satisfied teaching high school history."

He fell silent, and Francie thought about all the years she had heard the same thing from Greg. If he had been a whole man, she could have left him, but she had taken vows. For better or for worse.

No, Greg hadn't been the man she had married, but it also hadn't been his choice. That was what she had never been able to explain to Rafe, who had not known Greg the way he had been before. All those years, even when things kept getting worse, Francie had continued to search for some sign of the talented, ambitious young man who was trapped inside the vicious, ugly shell he had become.

"You said your ex-wife uses your name as a jab." Francie shifted so she could look at him more easily. "How could it be a jab?"

Alex was quiet for so long, Francie wondered if she had crossed a line. She was about to tell him not to worry about answering when he spoke.

"She can be brutal. No one's ever had the power to hurt me like she does, except my daughter."

"It's because we care what they think."

"I suppose so, though it shouldn't bother me anymore. When we first started dating, she thought Alex was short for Alexander, which fit her grand ideas. Alexander the Great and all that. Alexis, she thought, wasn't manly enough. She even nagged me for a while to get it legally changed."

"That's just stupid. Alexanders are a dime a dozen. I like Alexis. It's unusual."

"Do you think there's ever a second chance for people like us, Francie, with all our scars?" He lifted his hand and brushed a strand of hair from her face, leaving his palm on her cheek.

She reached up and ran her fingers down his cheek, rough with nearly a day's growth. A light smudge of dirt ran down one side, probably from when he had wiped his face while on the roof.

"There has to be, Alex." This time, she was the one to lean closer, touching her lips, feather-light, to his soft, warm ones. He pulled her closer, and he tasted like Cheberry.

His phone rang, and they jumped apart. Alex scrambled to pull it out before it quit ringing.

"Hey, Sam. You home already?" He stood and held the phone in place with his shoulder while he grabbed his jacket. Alex mouthed to Francie "My daughter," then talked back into the phone. "I've been helping a friend. You want to go to the grocery store?"

Francie got to her good foot while he struggled into his coat.

"Why do you need me to come along?"

When Francie took a hop toward the kitchen, he grabbed her shirt sleeve. "Where do you think you're going? No, I'm not talking to you, Sam. Hang on." He muted the phone.

"I was going to get the leftovers for you," Francie said.

"I'll get them." He unmuted his phone. "That's my friend, Sam. She sprained her ankle today . . . no, she's not from that dating site. Do you still have your Aircast from last year? Good. *Yes*, I want to come with you to the grocery store. I'm on my way now."

"I feel like I'm leaving you in the lurch." Alex put the phone in his pocket. "Do you need help getting to your room?"

Francie looked up the stairs and shook her head. "I'll sleep on the couch tonight. My foot's already feeling better after all that ice you kept putting on it."

He hurried into the kitchen and returned with a container. "I'll bring this back tomorrow with the Aircast."

"You don't have to—"

"Do you realize how often you say that? I *know* I don't have to." Alex leaned forward and kissed her cheek. "Thank you for a great day." He started walking backward toward the door. "Really."

Francie didn't move as he locked the door from the inside, closed it, and rattled the knob to make sure it was secure. The butterflies in her stomach were dancing the conga. If not for her ankle, her feet would have joined them.

Eight

lex woke early Sunday morning and lay in bed watching the sun rise. He couldn't remember when he had felt so good. The change in Sam the last week was nothing short of amazing. The phone call the night before saying she wanted to go shopping so she could cook had nearly floored him. She wanted to eat again. At the grocery store, she had chattered so much he could hardly get a word in. It was like the Before Sam was back. Her face had shone like she had a light shining inside her, like her gray world had suddenly seen the sun. He hoped it wasn't temporary.

Stretching, he glanced at the clock. He couldn't wait to get over to Francie's house again, but it might even be too early for her. The woman was simply amazing. The house was shabby but clean. How had she managed to work two jobs, care for an ailing husband, support a son preparing to go to Harvard, and maintain that incredible garden he had seen from the roof?

Thinking back on the day before, a desire to jump up and get to work flooded him. Francie needed his help. Alex grinned. She would fight him all the way, but he was ready for the battle.

Unable to stay in bed any longer, he got up. As he straightened the sheets, he wondered how she had done with her injured ankle, all alone. What if she had gotten up in the middle of the night and fallen? He hurried to the shower.

It wasn't until Alex was in the kitchen, collecting some things to take with him to Francie's, that he remembered he was supposed to meet *Destiny* that morning. All his anticipation drained away. He stood frozen in place with a package of steaks in one hand and a dozen eggs in the other.

A vision of Francie sitting at her well-worn table in her comfortable kitchen, laughing with him over dinner, came to mind. He didn't want to meet this *Destiny*; he wanted to make breakfast for Francie.

There wasn't time to do both. Alex eyed the meat. She was so proud. Would she be insulted if he showed up with the Aircast *and* some food, but couldn't stay? His gut told him she would. Kicking the bottom of the cupboard, he swore and put the meat and eggs back in the fridge. He only had enough time to drive out to her place with the brace.

The air was still crisp, and the colors in the trees seemed even more vibrant than they had the morning before. There were no signs of life as Alex drove past the front of the house. Was she still sleeping? Was she lying unconscious on the floor, out of reach of her phone?

He pulled up to the back porch, by the kitchen. The door was locked. Alex gave it a sharp rap and listened. No groans or cries for help. Was that water running? She was probably taking a shower. Relaxing, he took out his phone and sent her a text.

At your door with the Aircast. Want me to just leave it for you?

Pressing his ear to the door, he listened for her phone to announce his text. It did, and the sound of water stopped. Finally, his phone dinged with a reply.

Key under the mat

Releasing his breath, he bent over and felt underneath. He found the key easily. She needed a better hiding place.

Once inside, he paused. Alex could tell she had already been busy in the kitchen. The dishes he had left to dry had been put away. He listened for sounds of movement and thought he heard a door open.

"Francie, are you decent?" he called from the kitchen.

"I am now. You can come in."

He went into the living room. She stood by the downstairs bathroom door, dressed in faded jeans and a huge flannel shirt, a white towel wrapped around her head. Her skin seemed to glow. Makeup free, Francie watched him, a shy smile teasing the corners of her mouth. It wasn't just the beautiful old house that Alex found warm and comforting. Never, in all the time he and Vicki had been together, had it felt like this. He hadn't known it could.

"How did you sleep?" he finally asked.

"Pretty good, considering. I can put a little weight on my foot now." She took a cautious hobble toward him.

"Don't overdo it." He was by her side in two steps and pressed an arm to her waist for support. When she stumbled, he put his other arm under her legs and picked her up.

"Alex, I can do it myself."

"Of course you can." He carried her to the couch and put her down. "But you don't have to today." He grabbed the Aircast from where he had dropped it. "Let me see how this thing works for you. Made a huge difference for Sam."

"It's sure ugly." She sat with her arms folded across her chest as he lifted her leg and slid the brace over her foot.

"Now you're vain? It will support your ankle and make it easier to get around." He stood and reached his hands out to her. When she took them, he heaved her to her feet and moved a hand to her elbow. She smelled really good.

Cautiously, Francie stepped forward, leading out with her bad foot. She only paused a second before putting her full weight on it and taking another step. Then another and another.

"I can't believe what a difference this makes," she said.

"That's almost exactly what Sam said when she first put it on. I'm just glad it's the same foot she hurt."

"How are you doing?" Francie asked. When he looked confused, she pointed to his chest.

"Oh, that. I've had worse." Alex resisted touching the tender spot. The bruising had doubled in size over night. He checked his watch. "I have a date, uh, an appointment, so I need to get going." As soon as the words came out of his mouth he wished them back. Was that disappointment behind those beautiful dark eyes? Alex was tempted to change his plans right then.

"Well, thank you for bringing this by. You could have saved it for Monday."

"But you needed it today." Alex said. "Well, I'd better be off."

"Thanks again." She lifted her bad foot. "It really helps."

Alex pulled up to the little dog park where *Destiny* had suggested they meet. As soon as she had named the meeting place, he'd had reservations. Getting out of the car, he searched the area where people were already letting their pets run.

He liked dogs. A well-trained pet, given the right balance of discipline and affection, could be a wonderful family addition. His last dog had been killed five years before, hit by a car. Sam had named the beautiful Lab, Bubba, and neither Alex nor Sam had had the heart to fight Vicki about getting another pet. After the divorce, neither of them had had the heart for much of anything.

One of the dogs in the park took off with a growl after another one, the owners running and shouting after them. Yes, Alex liked dogs. He just didn't care much for them when other people trained them.

"Are you *KnightWeight*?" asked a high-pitched, almost little-girl voice behind him.

He turned around, and his eyes had to track up and up some more before he found the face of the tallest woman he had ever met, her blond hair hanging limply around her shoulders. Alex recognized *Destiny* from her profile picture. She held a tiny dog in her arms.

"Nice to meet you, Destiny." Alex held out his hand, and the dog snapped at it. He jerked his fingers out of reach.

"Stop it, Pikachu." *Destiny* looked Alex up and down. "You're short."

Alex squeezed the bridge of his nose and decided not to remind her that his profile stated his height. Besides, he was a good four inches taller than Francie.

"Have you given your dog a run yet?" he asked, trying to be pleasant.

"No." *Destiny* gave him another appraising look. "You won't do." Without another word, she lifted Pikachu to her shoulder, turned around, and walked away. From the woman's shoulder, the ugly little rodent snarled, its lip pulled back to show its teeth.

He stood for a few minutes leaning against the park fence. Glancing at his watch, Alex sighed. He kicked a rock and headed back to his car. Sam would be up by now, and she was cooking dinner.

Donna K. Weaver

Nine

lex whistled as he came down the stairs of his condo on Monday morning. The kitchen still smelled of Sam's experimental dinner the night before that had been quite good. Between Francie and Sam, Alex thought he must have eaten more eggplant over the weekend than he had all the rest of his life combined.

Sam was putting a bowl of oatmeal on the table, a steaming cup of herbal tea to the side. She was still dressed like a Goth in black synthetic pants, black blouse with lacy cuffs, and a mock leather vest, her nails freshly painted black, and her makeup neat but not overdone. He had to admit he must be getting used to it because he thought she actually looked quite nice.

"Good morning, Daddy."

"Morning, baby." Alex kissed her cheek then turned to the fridge.

"You were really busy Saturday."

"Yes, I was helping a hurt friend, remember?" Alex took two eggs from the carton and set them on the counter. "I wasn't going to tell you, but I had a date Sunday morning."

Sam sat with her spoon halfway to her mouth. When he didn't continue, she said, "And?"

"It was a disaster." As he cooked his breakfast, Alex told his daughter about the huge Amazon with the little-girl voice and a pet rat. Sam was laughing so hard by the end that she was crying.

"I'm sorry, Daddy. I shouldn't laugh." She wiped at her eyes. "Did she hurt your feelings?"

"No, but I'm going to cancel that stupid account."

Sam shot him a sly look before dropping her eyes.

"What are you up to?"

"You're not giving up on dating, are you?"

"I . . . I don't think so."

"Have you met someone?" Sam was suddenly alert, looking a little excited and a little alarmed at the same time.

"It's too early to tell," he said, eyeing her. "What are you doing that you're too busy to come by my office anymore?"

Sam wouldn't meet his gaze, and all her earlier happiness seemed to fade. So everything wasn't fixed.

Alex was at the office early. He had agreed not to delete his account, *yet*. He hadn't checked for new messages since accepting *Destiny's* invitation. Leaning back in his chair, he stared at the list of emails on his cell phone. He didn't have time to go through over a hundred.

In the outer office, he heard the door open. Francie was early. He jumped to his feet and went to the open door. She put her purse in the drawer and turned on the computer. Alex leaned against the jamb, watching as she stood and went to a file cabinet. She turned around and finally saw him.

"Look how well you're walking," he said. "Does it still hurt much?"

"Not much with the Aircast." She picked up the folders she would be working with that morning.

"Here, let me help you with those." Alex took them and walked with her to the copy room, holding the files in one hand and keeping a solicitous hand on her back.

"Were you able to get that canning done? I wish I could have helped you."

"I got a fair amount done. Do you like salsa?"

"I love salsa. Do you make it?"

"I did yesterday. It's a new recipe I downloaded. Do you mind being a guinea pig?"

"With *your* cooking? Any day." Alex found his mouth watering in anticipation.

Francie gave him a shy smile, her cheeks taking on a pretty flush. Her dark eyes caught him again, and he stumbled.

"You okay?" she asked, her hand on his elbow to help steady *him*.

"Stupid carpet." He scowled over his shoulder before turning back to her. "So you're experimenting with salsa?"

"I won't have much variety for Thanksgiving dinner, so I'm trying to come up with something I'm sure Rafe will like. I'm making some tonight, so I'll bring in a sample tomorrow."

"I can come and help. You already know I'm a good kitchen slave."

"You wouldn't mind?" They were at the copy room door, and Francie turned to face him.

"Not at all."

"The only pay I can give you is dinner."

"Stellar. What time?"

"Seven? I'll feed you then put you to work."

"I'll be there." Alex looked at his watch. "I have to get to class." He jogged back toward his office.

"What a hypocrite."

Passing Kevin's office, Alex almost missed the low comment. He stopped and took a couple of steps back to find Kevin in his office doorway, his hands in his pockets.

"What did you say?" Alex asked.

"You're nothing but a hypocrite, Diederik."

"What are you talking about?"

"I saw the way you were looking at our fair little assistant. You've got some nerve going postal on me, when you just wanted her for yourself." Kevin looked down the hallway, where the light from the open copy room door shone, then back at Alex. "I'm sure you've read her file and know she's a recent widow. I never knew you had it in you, going after the vulnerable ones. Is that why your wife left you?"

Alex almost hit him. He shoved his clenched fists to his sides, his blood pulsing so hard in his head that he could barely see. Kevin didn't say anything else, simply turned and went back into his office.

Francie hung up her cell phone, confused and disappointed. Had she misread Alex? Her cheeks went hot thinking of how she had kissed him on Saturday. She went over his reaction to her that morning. *He* had volunteered to come over to help *her*. In his call to say he wouldn't be coming that night, Alex had sounded odd, subdued. What had happened?

Francie picked up the little jar of jam she had brought for him. She put it on his desk before locking up and heading down the hall toward Professor Eldred's office. He was already in, so she kept quiet in case he was trying to work.

When Francie got up to file a paper, she was surprised to see him watching her from his doorway. Like Alex, but not like Alex. The way Professor Eldred was looking at her made Francie's skin crawl and brought back unpleasant memories. Her words to Rose about listening to her instincts came back.

Professor Eldred didn't say anything but turned around

and went back in his office, the corner of his mouth turned up in a smirk. She shivered. It was like he had taken a step back to that first day of school when he had made those disgusting comments about her to Alex.

Francie would have to rearrange the office. She reached into her purse and pulled out a bag that had a small mirror in it. No way was she going to let Eldred watch her from behind without her knowing it.

By Thursday, she just wanted the miserable week to end. Rose hadn't come to lunch once, but Francie knew the girl was at school because she had seen her go into Professor Eldred's office again early on Wednesday. Francie hadn't been able to stand guard, but she had called another assistant to come over.

Alex had done a complete turnaround since Monday morning. So much for being on a first-name basis. Now he didn't call her anything, and what little he did say to her was clipped. After giving the Aircast a thorough cleaning, she had put it in his office. Alex hadn't acknowledged it in any way. When he had left for a conference after his Wednesday morning classes, Francie had been relieved.

Then there was Rafe. He hadn't been there for their weekly call and hadn't replied to her message. He *always* returned her calls. Sitting in her bedroom that night, Francie had told herself Rafe had his own life, and she needed to leave him alone to live it.

On Thursday, when Francie sat down to lunch, she wondered what she was doing to drive away the people she cared about. She opened a book to do some reading but had barely read a paragraph when Rose plopped into the other chair. The girl didn't say anything and kept stretching as though watching for someone. Francie thought she looked tired.

"Have you ever had pumpkin soup?" Francie finally asked when Rose still hadn't spoken.

"Uh . . ." Rose glanced toward the cafeteria entrance where a new group of people stood talking.

"If you're too busy, it's all good." Francie packed up her trash, hoping Rose wasn't looking for Eldred.

"No, I haven't." Rose scooted her chair forward, giving Francie her full attention. "Can I come tonight? Pumpkin is my dad's favorite."

"Rose, is everything all right?"

For a minute, the girl looked like she might say something. At the last second, she squeezed her lips shut tight. Francie ached at the worry behind the girl's eyes.

"Well, let me know if there's anything I can do."

Rose nodded and turned again at the sound of some approaching students.

All that afternoon, Francie worried. The girl might as well be her daughter for all the time Francie spent fretting over her. Maybe Rose would open up over some pumpkin soup.

"Hey, you finally made it." Francie held open the kitchen door and hurried a shivering Rose inside.

"I know. I had to meet someone first. Brr. It's getting so cold outside." Rose's eyes darted to her purse at the familiar ring of a text message. She pulled her phone from it and checked it, almost sighing.

"Rose, I can tell something is wrong. Please, can I help?"

"I just have a lot going on right now."

The girl buried her face in her hands, but she wasn't crying. Was it frustration? Francie didn't push, but neither did she let it go, sitting still until Rose brought down her hands. Francie waited.

"I want to change my major," Rose finally said, throwing up her arms.

"Why is that a problem?"

"I don't think my parents will approve, though each for different reasons."

"Is it a scandalous major?" Francie tried to sound teasing, but Rose made a face.

"It would be to them, I think. To my mother, for sure." She dropped into a kitchen chair. "I want to study makeup artistry. I used to help with the high school plays, but I want to get good enough to do it for movies."

"Does ASU have a major for that?"

"No, but the University of Colorado in Boulder does." Rose's expression turned dreamy.

"So far away." Francie frowned. "How did you find out about it?"

"My aunt lives out there, and she has a neighbor who works at the college. Corky—that's the neighbor—was telling my aunt all about the Fringe Festival. Doesn't that sound incredible? Imagine *me* in a place where I'm not the weird one. I want to go there so bad."

"Does this Corky do anything with the festival?"

"I don't think so. Maybe it's her niece, Lisette, who does." Rose frowned. "No, it's not her. Corky just said something about Lisette having terrible taste in guys."

Francie perked up. The perfect segue. "Do you have a boyfriend?" Rose's head jerked toward Francie, and Rose almost looked scared. Francie took a deep breath to calm herself, surprised at the intensity of her desire to protect the girl. "Oh, honey, does he hurt you?"

"Wow, Francie. You look like you want to hit someone." Rose grabbed a napkin, her eyes wide.

"If your boyfriend's been hitting you, I just might."

"I don't have a boyfriend." Rose ripped little pieces off the napkin. "I want to tell you. I've wanted to all week, but it's not my secret to share." She tore the napkin in half.

"Don't worry, Rose." Francie patted the girl's hand and stood up. "I don't want you to betray a trust." Francie pulled out the roasted pumpkin from the fridge where it had been cooling.

"Oh, that smells so good." Rose jumped up and grabbed the apron she always wore. She came to stand beside Francie. "Do you have to use a whole pumpkin?"

"No, you can use the canned stuff, but this came from my garden. Why don't you dice an onion while I get the herbs going?" Francie pointed to a large stock pot on the stove. "I made vegetable broth for you."

"Thank you!" Rose gave her a quick hug before starting in on the onion. "All right," Rose said when she had finished slicing the onion. "I trust you, Francie, so I can tell you some of it. See, there's a girl in one of my classes who was seeing a professor."

"Just a guy who happens to be a professor, or one of *her* professors?"

"*Her* professor." Rose chopped the onion with an angry intensity. "When her mom died in the middle of the semester last spring, she got really behind in her classes. So, she comes to meet with this guy, and he makes her an offer." Rose wore one of those sage expressions she got sometimes, the ones that made Francie wonder what the girl had seen in her short life.

"And she took it?"

Rose nodded, picked up the cutting board, and headed toward the stove.

"Has she reported him?"

"She doesn't think she can; it would be his word against hers. He'd just say it was consensual." Rose used the knife to slide the onion pieces into the broth.

Francie felt sick as she stepped beside the girl to add the fresh thyme, parsley, and garlic to the pot. Her word against his. Francie remembered all too well the feeling of helplessness. At least she had only lost her job.

They went back to the table and started scooping the roasted pumpkin flesh into a food processor.

"That's all it takes?" Rose inhaled over the pot. "How did you cook the pumpkin?"

"You can roast it in the oven. I did it in the crockpot." Francie leaned against the counter and folded her arms. "It's Professor Eldred, isn't it?"

Rose spun to face her. "How did you know?"

"Remember, I work for him. What I want to know is why you keep going into his office when I'm not there. He's not supposed to do that."

"He's not supposed to be selling grades for sex either. Every time I go in there, I'm wired with a recorder. He's been coming on to me big time, and I have it all down. What I need is for him to offer me a better grade in exchange for putting out. I think I'm going to have to fail a couple of tests though. My grade's too high."

"You're incredible." Francie stared at the girl. "But honey, I don't think they'll admit that in court."

"They don't have to. Ever heard of the Internet?"

Francie burst out laughing, but she sobered quickly. "What if he says you doctored the file? He could sue you."

Rose's face went pale, and her shoulders drooped. "Are you kidding me? I've been putting up with Eldred's crap for nothing?" She flopped into a chair. "My dad teaches in the same department. I can't do anything that would hurt him."

"Do I know your father?"

"You must. Professor Diederik."

Francie's knees went weak, and she sat down.

"Are you okay?" Rose hurried around the table and knelt on the floor.

"You're Sam."

"Yeah." Her cheeks went red. Not looking at Francie, Rose—Sam—stood and went to the stove to stir the soup. "I guess you know my dad then?"

"I work for him *and* the snake." Francie pulled her phone from the other side of the table and sent a quick text to Alex, asking him to call her when he had a minute. "You said earlier that you trusted me. Why did you tell me your name was Rose?"

"It *is* Rose. Well, Rosamunde. It's my middle name, after my grandmother." Sam turned from the stove, clutching her hands to her chest as though she was praying. "See, when I tell people I'm Rose, I'm just Rose. Not Professor Diederik's daughter. Lots of students have taken classes from my dad. He's really popular. When they hear my last name, they act all weird, either because they think I'm too strange to be his daughter or because they're fans."

When Francie's phone rang, her heart did a little lurch. She put it on Speaker. "Hello."

"Hey, Ma. I'm so sorry I didn't call you back sooner. You wouldn't believe the week I've had."

Francie's throat had tightened at the sound of his voice, but she played it light. Letting out a shaky and exaggerated sigh, she said, "Well, it's begun. Out having fun while your aged mother languishes in solitude."

"Is that your son?" Sam giggled.

"Who's that?" Rafe asked. "Is that your friend, Rose?"

"Francie told you about me?" Sam's cheeks went pink with pleasure.

"Yeah, she has. Hey, Ma I—"

The phone vibrated, signaling another call, and Francie and Sam both jumped.

"So much for solitude, huh? Sounds like you have another call. I have to go anyway. Talk to you Sunday. Love you, Ma."

Francie fumbled to answer the second call.

"Francie, are you all right?" There was a lot of background noise; Alex must be at a restaurant.

"You need to talk to someone," Francie said, pushing the phone to the middle of the table. The sound of his alarmed voice made her stupidly happy. And he had used her first name.

"Daddy?" Sam's eye's darted between the little cell phone and Francie's face.

"What the . . . *Sam*? I can hardly hear. Was that Sam? Where are you?"

"She's at my house, Alex. She's the Rose I've told you about."

"Francie? Sam? Look, they're signaling to me. I'll call you in an hour." He hung up.

"You're your dad's lady friend." Sam clapped her hands. "He lent you my Aircast."

"I gave it back this week." Francie lifted the leg of her jeans to show the greenish, purpley bruise on her ankle.

"Ouchie." Sam sat in the chair beside Francie. "Did you guys fight or something? He was really happy for a couple of days, then, I don't know, it was like someone stole all the chocolate in the world."

"I have no idea what happened," Francie said then sniffed. "The soup!" She dashed to the stove, where she pulled the large pot off the burner. With a spoon, she stirred it, carefully running it over the bottom. *Like someone stole all the chocolate in the world.*

"Is it burned?" Sam asked at her side.

"I don't think so. One more thing to add then let it simmer a bit more." Francie opened the cupboard and removed a can of coconut milk. "Normally the recipe calls for cream."

"That's stuff's expensive. Did you buy it for me?"

"Don't worry about it." Francie opened the can and poured the smooth, white liquid into the dark, orange mass. "I've been collecting aluminum cans all summer, and I cashed them in."

"I've never known anyone like you before," Sam said. "I wish you were my mother."

"Don't say that."

Sam's eyes flashed, and Francie could see Alex in his daughter. "I don't like her." Sam's eyes went wide. "There. I said it." The girl stood taller, as though a huge load had been lifted from her thin shoulders.

"I'm sure your mother loves you—"

"And *I* love her . . . but I don't *like* her. Do you see the difference?" Sam started pacing the kitchen. "Seriously, if she wasn't my mother, I wouldn't have anything to do with her. I hate being around her. She's been pushing me to go with her to France." Sam made a gagging motion.

"Don't say bad things like that about her."

"Why shouldn't I? She says plenty of disgusting things about my dad."

"Please don't, Sam. Isn't name calling *her* style? I thought you didn't want to be like her."

"You're right." Sam stopped in front of Francie. "But if you're going to marry my dad, you need to know this."

"Your father and I aren't even dating," Francie said, her face going hot. "He's my boss."

Sam's eyes went wide again. "Is *that* the problem?" She nodded, answering her own question. "Yes, to my rigid, rule-keeping father, it would be. But it's obvious you two were made for each other."

"You've never seen us together, Sam. And it wasn't obvious to you an hour ago."

"*Yes*, it was. You have no idea how hard I've been working on him. Did you ever see that old musical *Hello, Dolly*? Well, Dolly's a matchmaker who has her eye on this old guy for herself, but she has to get him in a marrying frame of mind first. Since I met you, I've been getting my dad in the dating frame of mind." The girl shrugged. "I would love for you to be my mother."

"Sam, you are sweet to say that, but you're getting way ahead of things. The last time I saw your father, he looked like he could hardly stand the sight of me."

"Yeah." The girl shot Francie a knowing look, a single brow raised. "Just now on the phone he really sounded like he couldn't stand you."

"Let's eat," Francie said, feeling a little numb. "And you can tell me more about your plan to entrap Professor Eldred."

Donna K. Weaver

Ten

Alex used his keycard to get into the hotel room. His evening conference presentation had been a disaster; they would never ask him to present again. He didn't care; he was still trying to get his head around Sam and Francie knowing each other.

Shutting the door behind him, Alex leaned against it. He had listened to each of them talk about the other so often that he knew they were friends. Independent of him. If Sam was doing so well because of Francie, he owed his assistant more than she could possibly know. He grinned. As soon as Francie had said the name "Rose," he should have wondered if Sam was passing herself off as Rose again. This time, it didn't bother him.

Alex kicked off his shoes, took off his tie, and sat down to his laptop. Before he called back, he wanted to initiate something first. He paused, wondering if he was being presumptuous. The memory of Francie's kiss came to mind, as it had so many times over the last week—had it really only been a week? Alex couldn't be misreading her.

Taking his time to write the email, he paused and thought about all those stupid emails he had sent and received from that online site. It had always seemed risky to him, sending them out to random strangers. Francie was a risk he wholeheartedly wanted to take. Alex clicked Send.

He sat on the bed and hit autodial. Sam answered Francie's phone.

"Daddy! We just had the most heavenly pumpkin soup. I can't wait to make it for you. Or"—Sam's voice took on a sly note—"you should just try Francie's."

"Give me that phone, you minx."

He chuckled at the little struggle that ensued, with Sam cackling in the background.

"Hello," Francie said, when she finally got control of the phone.

"I have to study for a test, kids," Sam called from the background. "I'll leave you two to talk."

"Hang on," Francie said, and she must have put the phone down.

Alex could hear them talking but not much of what they were saying. Something about soup, secret Facebook groups, and YouTube. In a different time, with a different person, he might have been a little jealous of the connection between the two.

"I'm back." Francie sounded wary, and he didn't blame her. "I feel really stupid that I didn't realize Sam was Rose."

"Sam kept going on about this older lady who was teaching her cooking," Alex said. "I knew she liked you—whoever *you* were—but all this time I've been imagining a plump little grandmother with blue hair."

Francie didn't speak and, for a second, Alex wasn't sure what to say. Had he killed their easy camaraderie?

"I need to talk to you," Alex said.

"I'm listening."

"No. In person." He wished she would give him some encouragement. Her tone was so different from the teasing banter with Sam. "Can I take you to breakfast when I get back?"

Francie hesitated, and Alex held his breath. "I can make something," she finally said.

"I knew you'd say that. Let's work it out when I get there. Is that all right?"

"Sure."

"Well, good night, I guess."

"Night."

Alex tossed his phone to the bed. It was his own fault.

"You ready for breakfast?" Alex asked when Francie opened the kitchen door early Saturday morning. "I brought meat."

"I thought your flight back wasn't until tonight." Self-conscious in her shabbiest work clothes, Francie stepped back to let him inside. She took the flowers he handed her, not sure how to take his rather forced joviality.

"Took an earlier flight." He put his packages on the counter and turned to face her.

"Alex, what's going on?" Francie stood by the door, the bouquet still in her hands.

"Let's sit down, first, all right?" He came to her and held out his hand.

"I don't need help. My foot's almost as good as new." She brushed past him and sat at her table. "Thank you for asking."

"All right. I deserved that." He sat in the chair across from her. "Are you aware of the University's fraternization policy?"

"So Sam was right."

"Sam?"

Francie told him what his daughter had said the night before.

"After a coworker made a comment, I've been thinking about it all week."

"Eldred," Francie said, remembering when Alex had walked her to the copy room. Only that snake could have read anything in that.

Both of Alex's brows shot up. "How did you know? Well, it doesn't matter, Francie, he was right about one thing. As your direct supervisor, I have authority over you. I pulled out my copy of the school's policies and procedures handbook. The school doesn't like supervisors dating subordinates—there would be accusations of favoritism and undue influence."

"You should have just told me."

"Yes, I should have." Alex reached across the table, almost, but not quite, touching her hands. "But then I got to thinking about Saturday and wondering if you'd felt any pressure."

"Pressure?" Francie's cheeks grew warm. "*I'm* the one who kissed *you*, remember?"

"I'm not likely to forget it." The look he gave her made her cheeks grow even warmer. He covered her hand with his. "Look Francie, I want to get to know you, date you—even if it means losing you as my assistant."

Francie straightened. Was she going to lose her job?

"No, not that," Alex said, reading her expression correctly. "It's just up to the Dean to decide about shaking things up. He could move you to some other professors." Alex gave her a tentative smile. "Francie, I've already emailed the Dean about wanting to date you. Was I wrong to do that?"

"I . . . No." He had emailed the Dean about wanting to date her? Francie couldn't keep from smiling. "You weren't wrong,"

"Enough with all the legalese." Keeping her hand in his, Alex stepped around the table and pulled her into his arms. He ran his fingers lightly down her cheek then slid them along the side of her face, settling in the hair at the back of her neck. He leaned closer until his lips barely touched her cheek, making a tingling trail to the corner of her mouth.

"No pressure, Francie," he whispered, before finally finding her lips.

Donna K. Weaver

Epilogue

rancie wiped her hands on a dish towel for what must be the tenth time. She twisted again in front of the mirror. The vintage dress fit better than she had expected. Granny Gladys must have shrunk a lot as she aged. The black taffeta, knee-length evening dress still had a hint of moth balls, but Francie hoped her cologne was enough to cover it.

It felt strange to be dressed up. She hadn't worn anything like Gran's dress since senior prom. Francie had done her best to put up her hair by herself, wishing all the time that it wasn't Sam's weekend with her mother. The girl had such flair, Francie was sure she could have done something amazing with it. After adjusting the shawl-like bodice of the dress and straightening the only nice necklace she owned, Francie couldn't see anything else to fix. Her reflection was as good as she got.

As she walked down the stairs in the fancy heels she had bought for the first day of school, Francie thought back over everything that had happened since the beginning of the semester. She mentally checked off what she had accomplished, including maintaining a 3.5 GPA so far—stupid remedial math—and doing well in her first office job. Alex and Sam.

An immense sense of peace settled over Francie. Considering all she'd had to overcome, what she had done *was* kind of amazing. For the first time in years, she accepted—deep in her heart—that she was worthwhile. Greg had been wrong, and Alex was right.

Alex. Francie let out a happy sigh and looked down at her shoes again. When she had bought them just a few months ago, she hadn't even thought about Gran's dress. Francie was happy it wasn't supposed to snow until tomorrow, so she could wear them.

It wasn't long before Alex's headlights came up the drive. He stopped in front of the house—so much more formal than going to the back door like usual. Francie's nerves went all aflutter again, and she wished she had thought to bring the hand towel with her.

Keeping out of sight behind the living room drapes, she watched him get out of the car. She loved doing that, watching when he didn't know it. Before shutting the door, he paused in the light to straighten his tie. A bow tie. And he carried a single red rose.

What had Francie done for life to be so good now? Because she feared it could all go away again, she had been savoring every moment. Thinking back on that day in the cemetery before Rafe went off to school, she felt like a different person.

A sharp rap on the door announced Alex. Taking a deep breath, she opened it, then paused, drinking him in. She loved how the soft porch light reflected off the gray at his temples. His laugh lines crinkled as he checked her out.

"Wow, Francie," he said, his voice soft.

"Come in." She pushed open the screen door.

"Let me see you in the light." He took her hand and pulled her to the center of the living room, where a pool of light from the bright kitchen shone. Alex mumbled something and went around the living room, turning on every light. "That's better. You look incredible." Alex's eyes blazed, and for a second she thought he might kiss her, but he bowed instead and presented her with the rose, then offered her his arm.

During the drive, Alex made casual conversation. It wasn't like him, so Francie decided he must be up to something. Just the thought of what it might be made her chest ache. He had obviously gone to a lot of work, and she didn't want to spoil whatever it was by guessing wrong then being disappointed.

Alex pulled into the Vidalia parking lot. Even though it wasn't Thanksgiving yet, the place was already decorated for Christmas, with strands of white lights wrapped tightly around the tree branches. Francie let out her breath.

"I thought you might like it," he said.

"I've always wanted to eat here. From the website, the food presentation is beautiful."

Once again, he offered her his arm, and they walked in together. There was a decent line of people, and Francie's heart sank. She thought it would take at least an hour to get all of them seated in the smallish restaurant.

"Don't worry," Alex said, when she tightened her grip on his arm. He turned to the greeter. "Reservation for four under Diederik."

"Sure, Professor." The young woman shot Francie an odd look. "The other members of your party are already seated. If you'll come with me."

"Four?" Francie whispered as they followed her.

"You'll see."

Walking past the brick columns into the dining area, Francie fought against her sagging spirits. A work dinner?

She didn't mind going with Alex to them, but after his request for her to wear a fancy dress and him showing up in a bow tie, Francie wished she had known the evening *wasn't* something special.

A few of the customers greeted Alex or raised hands in acknowledgment of him, casting her interested glances. She even recognized her new bosses sitting with the professor who had replaced Kevin Eldred when he had resigned last month. Francie had been so proud of the way Sam had staged a quiet confrontation between the man and three of his victims—all captured on video.

They came around a corner. At the table sat two young people caught up in an animated conversation.

"Rafe!" Francie gasped.

He turned at the sound of his name and leapt from the chair to pull her into a huge hug. Francie couldn't believe how much taller he seemed. She reached up to touch his cheeks, checking to make sure they weren't hollow.

"Ma." He laughed. "I'm eating enough." Rafe reached behind her and shook Alex's hand. "It's great to see you again, sir."

Again? Francie turned to Alex. He had his other arm around Sam, who bubbled with excitement, a hint of a smile tugging at the corner of his mouth. His gaze had an intensity that took Francie's breath away.

"Let me fix your makeup." Sam grabbed a napkin and went to work on Francie's eyes.

"I can't believe you kept this a secret," Francie whispered.

"You, of all people, should know better."

"When are you going to tell your father about your role in all that?" Eldred's resignation had surprised everyone in the department but Francie, and even she didn't know many of the details. The whole thing had been very low key.

"Not my secret to share, remember? Or yours." Sam

leaned in and whispered, "Why did you never mention you have a hunk for a son?" She didn't wait for an answer but backed up, pulling on Rafe's suit jacket so he stepped back beside her.

Francie frowned, her pulse quickening. Beside her, Alex moved, and she turned to find he had dropped to one knee. A thrill went through her body as she realized his intent, here, in front of all these people.

On some level, she sensed Sam and Rafe watching them, people rising from the nearby tables, of camera's flashing. All Francie could see was Alex's face. He reached up and took her hand, his warm fingers curling around hers.

"Rafe," Alex said, his eyes never leaving Francie's. "Do I have your permission to marry your mother?"

"You do, sir." Rafe's voice rang out, sure and strong.

Francie's hand shook in Alex's, and he pressed it tighter, the corner of his mouth turning up. "Sam, would you like me to marry Francie?"

"Yes, yes, yes!" Sam jumped up and down, squeezing Rafe's arm.

"Francie, I love you." Alex's voice was low. He reached into his pocket and pulled out a small box which he flicked open with his thumb. "I want to spend the rest of my life with you. Will you marry me?"

"Oh, yes, Alex. Yes." She could hardly get enough breath to speak.

Cameras flashed, and people cheered. Rafe stepped over to hold the box, so Alex could remove the ring. He slid it onto her finger and stood. Never breaking eye contact, he pulled her into his arms.

"I love you too, Alex." Francie put her arms around his neck and, heedless of the audience, lifted her lips to meet his.

The End

Author's Note
& a Free Book

Dear Reader,

Thank you for taking the time to read *Second Chances 101*. There are so many book options out there that I feel privileged you chose my book.

If you enjoyed it, I would be thrilled to have you leave a review on Goodreads or Amazon or anywhere else you share your thoughts on books.

I also love to hear from readers. You can find me on Facebook, Twitter, my blog at donnakweaver.com, or you can email me at donnakweaver@gmail.com.

Turn the page to find instructions on how you can get a free book!

Thanks!
Donna

Hope's Watch

Book 1.5 in the *Safe Harbors* Series

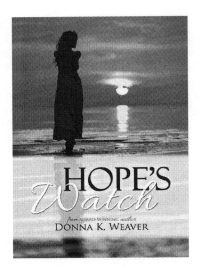

Elle Reinhardt is filled with emotional wounds from a ship excursion gone wrong that ended in death and disaster at the hands of modern-day pirates. As grieving loved ones wait for news of those lost at sea, she tries desperately to buoy them up.

Malcolm Armstrong, friend of one of the missing men, arrives to act as family spokesman. Elle knows it's unreasonable, but she resents his presence. When Mal offers the strength she so desperately needs, will she be able to let go of her animosity and accept his support?

This ebook novelette includes excerpts from both *A Change of Plans* and *Torn Canvas*.

Receive the **FREE** book Hope's Watch, Safe Harbors #1.5 and updates on new releases by typing this link into your browser: **http://eepurl.com/cb_80z**

A Change of Plans

Book 1 in the *Safe Harbors* Series

Lyn wants to move on. She just doesn't realize it will take pirates, shipwreck, and an intriguing surgeon to do it.

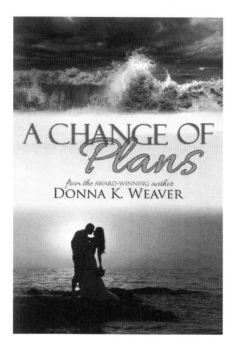

"Ms. Weaver pens an outstanding, epic tale of life, loss, and love! ... There are truly no words to describe how solid and endearing Lyn and Braedon are ... Their love grips the reader and doesn't let go for a second ... Ms. Weaver has created magic!" - Mimi Smith, *InD'Tale Magazine*

Torn Canvas

Book 2 in the *Safe Harbors Series*

*Winner of the prestigious RONE award
for best New Adult Fiction.*

Sometimes even a hero needs rescuing …

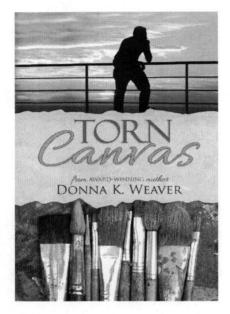

"A fantastic work of fiction... Jori is no longer the confident skirt-chasing model, but a man haunted by his scars. His journey of self-discovery ... helps him grow as a person and an artist... An absolute must read!" Sarah E. Bradley, *InD'Tale* Magazine

A Season of Change

Book 2.5 in the *Safe Harbors* Series

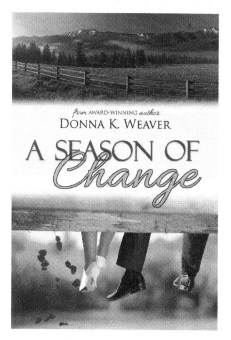

It's a time of change for Jori Virtanen. The former playboy model is about to be married. He juggles wedding arrangements, a bachelor party, and plans for keeping the ceremony secret from the press. But Jori has another problem. He has to figure out how to tell one of his best friends, Marc North, that his girlfriend may not be what she appears.

A Savage Ghost

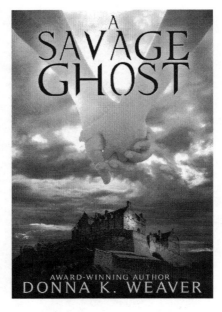

Lia Savage reluctantly puts her dream of opening a dessert boutique on hold to help her dad remodel a castle he's inherited in Washington State. Soon, a specter targets her younger sister.

Lia enlists the help of strapping Coop Montgomery, the head gardener and her former crush. As they search together for a way to rid the castle of its ghost, the romance she used to dream about with Coop kindles. But Lia's gentle giant means to stay in Washington while she's determined to return to California. She must find the courage to face both the ghost and her future.

With Coop. Or without him.

Acknowledgements

As always, I'd like to thank my husband for his patience when I bury myself in my writing--even during the first week of our 30th anniversary cruise. I appreciate the input from my Pied Piper critique partners Meredith, Nanette, Marla, Donea, and Ken. I'd like to send a huge thanks to my fellow Ripple Effect authors for letting me come along for the ride.

About Donna K. Weaver

Award-winning author, wife, mother, grandmother, Army veteran, karate black belt, Harry Potter nerd, online gamer.

40596200R10073

Made in the USA
Middletown, DE
17 February 2017